definitely not a thing

christina c jones

man...

It feels like it has been so, so long.

It's been tough.

Since my mom passed (on Inauguration Day, mind you, I like to believe she was like, *"actually, for real for real, fuck Donald Trump"*), every word has been a struggle - we're already nearly at the end of the year, and this is only the second project I've been able to bring to completion.

I had *such* grand plans.

Finishing and starting series, events, merch releases, all that.

Grief said, "lol bye."

So instead of any of the stuff I was "supposed" to be writing, the stuff I planned to write... I set off to have fun.

No real expectations, just a silly little crumb of a plot very loosely based on something ridiculous I saw in my real life neighborhood Facebook group.

Thus, Calvin and Amelia were born.

It's warm, and fun, and light.

It's *so* light.

And I hope that does something for you.
Happy reading!

1 /
amelia

IF YOU ASKED ME – with full recognition that no one did, actually – fatalism was a character flaw. Like it was actually wild to me to wake up with movement in your limbs, breathe in your lungs, and logic in your mind, and *not* be able to find anything to be positive about.

However.

I would be a liar if I pretended that, at this particular juncture of my journey, I didn't understand and unfortunately relate to the age old adage of:

Fuck my life.

Like… I felt that shit.

Real bad.

"You already back? That was quick!" Arthur cackled from the front stoop as I hopped down from the elevated seat of the moving truck. My gaze cut in his direction, finding his eyes under the weathered brim of the *Arthur's Refrigeration* cap he thought hid his premature balding.

"Literally shut the fuck up!" I yelled, wiping the goofy grin off his face.

Okay.

Fine.

1

I didn't actually say that.

I really, *really* wanted to though.

Instead, I settled on, "Mind your business," which only generated more – annoying ass – laughter as I trudged up the front steps of the building with a box of immediate essentials under my arm and a set of unfamiliar keys in the opposite hand.

He did at least open the door for me.

I ignored his commentary as he did that "favor", knowing that if I engaged, the chances of me crashing out were through the stratosphere.

I was determined to be cool.

I was cool.

Everything was cool.

Why wouldn't things be cool?

What *wasn't* cool about getting broken up with by a man you'd moved in with less than six months ago, signing a lease for your dream brownstone only for it fall through because of construction issues, forcing you to move back into the same building as your ex?

Your own unit, though.

So… it was cool.

It was so, *so* fucking cool.

Icy, even.

Fuck my life.

The "new" unit was on the second floor, so I didn't even bother waiting for the elevator – I took the stairs up, hoping that the music radiating through the building would be somewhere in the distance.

Which, was probably where I went wrong.

Because why would I hope that?

Why would I think it would work out in that way for me?

Why wouldn't the loud, explicit version of goddamn *Splash Waterfalls* be coming from right next door to the apartment I was supposed to be moving into?

No reason.

Because it was.

With the door open, and people loitering in the hall with red solo cups in their hands, looking at me like *I* was the crazy one for daring to try to get through.

Of course this was the way this turned out.

Of course it was.

"Ay, you need help with that?" I heard, from somewhere above me but not the voice I carried in my head for God.

Out of nowhere, hands were on the box I'd been carrying, "helping" take the load off.

Now, admittedly, it was hella heavy, and the corner pressed into my thigh had been bearing most of the weight and almost certainly creating a bruise, so it actually *was* a relief.

Physically.

Mentally, emotionally, *primally*, though?

"What I need is for y'all to get out of the way and stop making all this damn noise!"

Okay.

Fine.

I didn't actually say… oh.

Shit.

Did I actually say that?

If I had to judge based on the dirty looks from the folks in earshot in the hall, and the screwed-up face that belonged to the "helping" hands…

Yeah.

I said it.

3

And I meant it.

I just like... didn't mean to say it.

"Oh. That's whassup," the deep voice from above said, unceremoniously shifting the weight of the box back into my arms – back to my arm. *Not* my leg, where I'd actually been carrying it, which resulted in an embarrassingly un-immediate drop to the floor.

Thank the lord I believed in good tape.

Instead of all the box contents spilling out, it simply hit the ground with a resounding *thump* that brought any attention that *hadn't* been pointed my way... pointed my way.

Wonderful.

"I didn't mean to say that!" I called in the direction of my "helper", who was long gone by now. I put on the tight smile of someone who'd run into a coworker, retrieved my box, and continued my journey a few more feet, to the door of the place I'd be calling home for the next few months.

At least, that's what Chase – the realtor -had claimed the timeline was.

We'd see.

Only because of the way the rest of the day had been going was I concerned about what the apartment was going to look like. I'd lived in the building for six months already, and before that, had been coming and going and staying over with my ex for years.

Two, to be precise.

It wasn't a perfect building by any means – *The Foundry* was historic, and constantly being renovated, with the style of each unit controlled by whoever rented the place at the time. The concept was actually quite cool, and one of the reasons I'd been sad to move out.

Besides the whole *relationship of two years going kaput* of it all.

I was *supposed* to be moving into a gorgeous restored townhouse though.

I would be moving into that gorgeous restored townhouse.

In three months.

Surely I could avoid *one* man in a ten-unit building for three months, right?

Inside the apartment, I was pleasantly surprised to find that the unit's previous tenant had kept with lots of the original features – exposed brick, exposed ceiling beams, plaster walls. Back then those choices had been money-saving moves rather than aesthetic choices, but it was beautifully on trend *now*.

It wasn't my townhouse, but it would do just fine.

I took a look around, checking faucets, switches, hinges, drains, corners and crevices, making sure everything worked as it should and that I wouldn't have any surprise wildlife encounters. Once I was satisfied with that, I plopped down on the hardwood of my temporary living room, with my box. Using my keys as a knife, I popped the tape and began removing the things I'd determined I would need for the night without having to unpack the van.

A change of clothes.

Toiletries.

Blow-up mattress.

Linens.

Chargers for my electronics.

My laptop.

My journal and pen.

A few bottles of water.

Snacks.

Anything else I might need was either already in the truck I'd borrowed or another quick *Proxy* order away thanks to the cell phone in my pocket.

I spent the next thirty minutes showering and getting comfortable, then the thirty after that setting up my little spot on the floor, then checking in on work items I'd been unfortunately neglecting. Proxy itself was my baby, a whole small – but succesfull!—business I was responsible for. The last week of my life had been spent in a tailspin – one I needed to re-route before it veered too far off course.

Which… obviously easier said than done.

Especially when…

Shit.

Was I really about to admit to myself, finally, that I was actually…

… *hurt?*

Oh.

Okay.

According to the sudden, fresh prickle of tears in my eyes… yes.

Yes, I was.

As much as I hated that it was the case, the unexpected end of a nearly three year relationship was *not* something I could simply brush off and easily move on from – at least, that's what the logical parts of my brain were processing.

Had *been* processing.

I'd been moving on autopilot really, as soon as I realized my new reality. I'd found a new place immediately – and it felt quite serendipitous for my *dream* place to be available right when I needed it. I packed my shit, ignored the *maybe we should talk about this more* pleas, and got my ass on.

And now I was back.

Unfortunately.

I blew out a sigh and closed my laptop, knowing that work was out of the question now that I'd let myself travel down this emotional path. I put my earbuds in instead, turned the lights and temperature down, got under my blanket and closed my eyes while Sza crooned in my ears.

Perfect self-loathing vibes.

I *hated* being fatalistic, really.

I thrived on finding the positive, getting things done despite the barriers, blah, blah, blah.

But man... this was really, *really* fucked up.

I would get through – *what the fuck is that?*

I sat up on my mattress, squinting as if it would help me hear better. From somewhere – likely next door – I could literally *feel* the bass reverberating. I glanced at my phone to check the time – approaching midnight, which was *well* past the nine-o-clock noise rule.

I groaned as I weighed my available options. I didn't want to move in and immediately start the Karen antics, but I could barely hear my *own* music directly in my ears over theirs.

That was just egregious.

With that in mind, I neatly removed a page from the back of my journal, taking a moment to scribble a quick note.

Hi neighbor! It's quite late, and the music is quite loud – any chance we can make some adjustment? Thank you!

Was it the most polite?

No.

7

But it wasn't as rude as it could be, considering *they* were bothering *me.*

Instead of knocking, I slid the note under the door – surely somebody from the party would find it and deliver to whoever the actual tenant was.

I was barely back inside my apartment when the music stopped completely, bringing a smile to my face.

"Thanks, neighbor," making a mental note to formally introduce myself the next day, to make sure there weren't any weird vibes.

My earbuds went back in, sad music on, covers tuck— WHAT THE FUCK IS THAT.

I sat straight up, again, as Big Sean repeated *"Ass, Ass, Ass,"* over and over – the chorus of his song colloquially known by the same damn name.

Somehow, it was *louder* than before.

Oh.

Oh.

I hopped right back out of the bed, grabbing my keys and cell to stow in my pockets before I stomped out of my apartment back into the hall.

This time, I *did* knock, like I was the police at that.

I was *not* an angry, confrontational kinda girly, but *this?*

"You're about to see a motherfucker hammer time," I grumbled under my breath, hands propped on my hips as I waited for somebody to answer the door.

I had my fist poised to knock again when it swung open, putting me eye-to-nipple with a man who started the interaction with a condescending chuckle.

"Damn – you mad as *fuck,* huh?" he laughed more, as I tipped my head back to really see him.

Why the *fuck* would he be this fine?

8

Smooth brown skin, strong jaw, wide nose, lots of thick, healthy hair – on his head *and* face.

Was that necessary?

Fineness aside, my brows furrowed even harder. "Yes, actually – you're being rude."

He scoffed, then used the phone in his hand to stop the music. *"I'm* rude? Ms. *Get out my fucking way and shut up?"*

My mouth dropped open. "I did *not* say all that!"

He shrugged – broad, tattooed, cinnamon brown shoulders. "May as well have."

"Maybe so, but I didn't, and I didn't even mean to say anything."

"But you did though, and it was rude, so…."

"So… I deserve to not get any sleep because you're having a party?"

"The party is over."

I peeked around him, and it did indeed appear that his guests had left.

"Oh – you're being loud and obnoxious just for fun, then?"

His full lips spread into a little smirk. "Thanks for understanding."

Before I could reply, he'd started the music back up, and was about to close the door until I put my hand up, stopping it.

"Hey – can you… just… *not?"* I asked, with a huff. "Look – I'm sorry for being rude in the hall earlier. I had —*have*—a lot on my mind."

"Ohhh, you've got a lot on your miiiind," he droned, and I had to bite the inside of my lip to keep a rude comment from spilling out.

Shit.

9

*Maybe I **am** rude?*

"You know... have a good night," I said instead of what I wanted to say, and turned to walk back to my own door.

I would simply let HPD handle it, as much as I didn't want to go there.

"You too," he called after me, laughing as I went back into my apartment.

I wanted to scream.

Hell, maybe I should.

Who would hear it anyway, with *Ass* on full blast?

Fuck it.

I braced myself, and let out a full volume, full throated scream, channeling every molecule of rage I was feeling into the sound. I half expected it to not even be satisfying, with the music drowning it out.

Except.

There was no music drowning it out.

It was deathly quiet, in fact, the perfect scenario for my insane rage-scream to echo through the empty apartment, repeating back to me with embarrassing clarity.

And then, moments later... a knock at my door.

Since I was still standing there, I simply turned around to unlock and open it.

My neighbor stood there, shirtless and smirking.

"Hey... you think you could maybe keep it down?"

2 /
amelia

ONE OF THE greatest poets of our time once posed a question, with options to decipher a worst case scenario.

Looking jealous.

Looking crazy.

Looking jealous *and* crazy.

Being walked all over.

I was at risk of all four, and right on the verge of crashing out because of it.

I could've written the night before off as one-time-insanity, a cascade of unfortunate coincidences that just compounded on each other, never to be experienced again.

Until I was woken up at the exposed ass-crack of dawn to the sound of *something* heavy being dropped on the floor, rhythmless but constant – just enough space between to not tune it out as it vibrated my floors.

That was *one* of the issues with these older buildings, and part of why I'd wanted a single unit – there was very little protection from the noise pollution of your neighbors. I'd noticed it when I lived with Hunter, and it had been annoying then, but I was too in love for it to matter.

11

It was wild how one little *"wait, I didn't mean it like that"* statement had so instantly dried me up – pussy, heart, common sense, all of it.

Cold fucking turkey.

Feelings I *really* needed to process, but couldn't, when the guy next door kept dropping his weights – it finally clicked for me – on the ground.

Killing his floors, but whatever.

Wasn't my apartment.

On the bathroom sink, my phone buzzed, and I grabbed it with the hand that wasn't occupied navigating my toothbrush around my mouth to read the text.

"Hey my baby. How was the first night? – Kae"

I cringed at the text as immediate embarrassment flushed through me, heating my face. Kaelynn was one of my best, like *best* friends, known her since we were literal babies, and still… that scream situation was crazy, and still super fresh on my mind.

"Uh… no comment," I typed back, already knowing that wasn't actually going to work, but buying myself a couple of minutes before I had to explain.

Sure enough, the response I got back was the wide-eyed blush emoji, followed up immediately by the nosy eyes.

I sighed, finished brushing my teeth, then hit the button to connect a video call as I grabbed my cleanser from the toiletry bag on the counter.

"No comment is craaazy," was the first thing out of Kae's mouth when the call connected. She was clearly on a beach somewhere, and wearing shades, but they weren't so tinted I couldn't see the concern in her eyes.

"Nothing happened – not *really*," I assured her to ease her mind. "Just… embarrassing shit."

"You already ran into Hunter?" she guessed, sitting up to get closer to the screen, and I shook my head.

"No – thank *God*," I mused. "I've actually been thinking… should I unblock him to tell him I'm in the building? So it's not some weird surprise?"

"Hell no," Kae immediately shot back. "I mean, will it be awkward, sure – but you're at least expecting it to happen. He isn't. he's going to shit himself when he sees you there, it'll be great."

"Great?" I laughed, shaking my head as I massaged the cleanser into my skin. "We might have different definitions of that."

"Great in a *fuck you* kinda way," she explained.

"In a fuck *me* kinda way."

"Fair enough – both of you, but him just a *little* more, which is good enough for me. Because… well… fuck him," she shrugged, sitting back. "He better be glad I'm not in town. I see he waited for me to be gone to act up."

I frowned as I flipped the water on to rinse my face. "I don't know if *act up* is the correct term, so much as, *finally got honest.*"

Kae huffed. "Fine. Either way. I'm punching him in his shit next time I see – girl *what* is that noise? Is maintenance doing something in your apartment?"

I gave her a dry, wet smile. "Actually, that is my neighbor trying to set off the lunk alarm next door."

"Wait, huh?" she asked. "Like lifting weights? And it's loud like that?"

"Right. There's zero noise insulation in these historic buildings, but… he might be making extra noise on purpose honestly."

She raised an eyebrow. "Why would he be making noise on purpose?"

13

I blew out a sigh, grabbed the next step in my skin routine, and launched into the whole story from yesterday – from Arthur being annoying to my ill-fated scream. She listened without a single interruption – or reaction, at that.

And then…

She bursted out laughing.

Like… literal tears streaming down her face laughing.

"Kaelynn, it's *not* that damn funny."

"I'm *so* sorry Ames, but it very much is," she countered, wiping her face. "Why are you in that building being an asshole?"

"*Me*?!" I asked, and she nodded.

"Yes, *you*," she laughed. "Like he's definitely being petty but what would you expect after being mean when he was trying to help you?!"

"Girl I'm about to hang up."

"*Nooo*," she cackled. "Don't hang up!"

"Why the hell not?"

"Because you love me."

"And it is clearly not reciprocated because *why* are you on his side and not mine?"

Kae gasped. "Why would you think that?!"

"You are literally *cackling* at my pain!"

"You delivered it *very* comedically!" she defended, still laughing, but then her expression shifted, and she blew out a deep sigh. "Okay. I'm done laughing, and ready to support you through this challenging transition."

"You make me *so* sick," I giggled. "It's… it's just a break up? Right? I'll be fine."

She nodded. "You will be fine, definitely. But… you ain't gotta fake the funk with me – as a matter of fact, please don't," she amended. "You're hurt, and that's okay.

14

More than, in fact. You were with Hunter for damn near three years – that nigga talked to me about rings, it wasn't some shallow thing. You don't have to try to be over it in a week."

Kae was right.

Unquestionably.

But... I was stuck, mid-pat of moisturizer, on... "he talked to you about rings?"

Immediately, Kae's face dropped. "*Shit,*" she muttered under her breath. "Ames, I—"

"It's fine," I interrupted, shaking my head as I finished with my face. "I mean... why should that be surprising, that far into a relationship, you know? I just... I don't understand how that falls in line with not being sure. Like how the fuck are you not sure, but talking to—you know, whatever. *Whatever.*"

"Clearly he was all over the place," Kae said, pulling her shades off. "And if it matters at all, I kinda told him that when he brought it up to me."

"Told him what?"

"To not play in your face by giving you a ring if he wasn't really there with it."

I frowned. "So you knew he was iffy?"

"I didn't *know* anything... but like... neither did he, if that makes sense," she answered. "The conversation just had a little too much... *maybe,* and *I think,* versus... *I know.* And it was like a year ago – before you agreed to move in. It didn't seem abnormal to me, just maybe too soon?"

"It's been three years."

She shrugged. "That's not that long these days. And we're still young."

"I'm thirty-four. He's thirty-six."

"Do you think that's old?"

15

"In general? Of course not," I said. "But *too* old I think for age to be like... an excuse to not... to be... shit, I don't know."

Kae frowned. "Bitch me either – we're in the same single ass streets."

"Yeah, and there's no one I'd rather start a fresh hoe-phase with, but damn... I was *not* anticipating ever taking another dip in the – famously – pissy dating pool. *Not* that I'm anywhere near ready for that," I quickly added.

The idea of it made my stomach hurt, actually.

"The last thing I want to do is waste my time again," I mused. "If I'd known... if I'd heeded the red flags, instead of just *going with the flow*... ugh." I sighed. "There's not a point in lingering on it, but like I said... I'm good on niggas for a little while, at least."

"So we're on the same page then," Kae said. "You don't have to be ready for anything – you just have to be real with yourself about what you're feeling, and where you are."

I raised an eyebrow. "An air mattress in an empty apartment in the same building as my ex, next door to a man who probably thinks I need a grippy sock vacation and is actively trying to drive me into a psychotic break?"

Kae laughed. "Day one of Amelia's Healing Journey!"

"You're an asshole."

"An incredibly gorgeous, smooth one," she crooned at the screen, making me laugh. "Love you."

"Love you too," I replied as we transitioned off the call.

As soon as there was silence in the apartment again... there was another loud clang.

And a grunt.

"You are way too pretty for jail," I told myself in the

16

mirror, then picked up my phone again, navigating to the *Proxy* app. I'd already used the app to schedule help getting the truck unloaded, but I needed to check just one more time to be sure.

Good.

I was confirmed, and my timeframe wasn't until early afternoon, so I had time to get some things done. I got dressed, put the mattress and my other things away, then grabbed my laptop and bag to head to Urban Grind.

Usually, I worked from home, but an empty apartment wasn't quite "home" yet.

Although... this one was already more *home* than I'd ever gotten to feel at Hunter's place, having to field his input on every little thing – and conceding to his opinion nearly every time -- despite the place being supposedly *ours*.

But, whatever.

I spent a few minutes before stepping out the door on morning greetings via text with family and friends and then stepped out into the hall, ready to make it a great day – or, at least as good as possible.

So obviously the first thing I saw – nay, *walked into* – was bags of trash right next to my door.

The rage was *so* immediate it kinda scared me.

Walking around pissed off was simply *not* my default, and it was annoying at this point, actually.

I blew out a cleansing breath, letting logic prevail.

There was a party last night – of course there was trash to be taken out.

Multiple bags.

The dumpster for the building was a bit of a trek, so *of course* someone might stow them outside the door for a

17

bit while they made sure they had them all, so they could try to make just one trip.

This was no big deal.

And had nothing to do with me.

This was not an issue, or my problem at all – I was leaving right now anyway, to go have a great day!

I plastered a smile on my face and started walking, glancing up as the door next to mine swung open while I was passing.

"Good morning," I greeted, in the brightest tone I could fine as my neighbor stepped out of his door.

"Ah, Scream Queen – whassup?"

Immediately, the smile slid off my face, and all my faux-positive energy oozed out through my feet.

"Nothing much... mister... uh... *Noise Violation*," I countered, the only thing I could bring to mind in enough time to not be awkward.

A little smirk spread over his lips as he stepped a bit closer – salty and sweaty from whatever workout he'd been doing earlier, glistening like a damn sports drink commercial. *"Noise Violation*, huh?"

"That's what I said!" I shot back, indignant – which, really only seemed to be even more amusing to him. "Are you finished with the petty payback now?"

He chuckled as he turned to grab his trash bags, tatted muscles flexing ever-so-slightly from the effort. "You think I'm being petty?"

"That's the generous read on your behavior thus far, yes," I replied as he turned to face me again.

"What's the not-so-generous one?"

I bit my lip, thinking about it for a second before I shrugged. "That you're just an asshole, and it has nothing to do with me at all."

"Oh, it's got *everything* to do with you, neighbor."

I rolled my eyes. "Oh, am I at least *neighbor* now? Not *Scream Queen?*"

"I'll table that nickname unless you make it a habit."

"Screaming is *not* a habit of mine," I countered, and he raised an eyebrow at me.

"I can tell. Maybe that's the problem," he suggested with a wink, then started for the elevator while I stood there trying to figure out what the hell that me—

"Okay fuck you!" I called after him as the elevator closed.

3 /
amelia

A TRIP to Urban Grind *always* hit the right note for me.

Every.

Freaking.

Time.

I got myself there early enough to get my preferred, perfect little spot in a cozy chair next to the window, got a latte and a pastry, and locked in on things with Proxy.

The technical side of things was largely over my head – at least where the coding and databases and cyber security of it all were concerned. Ideas and implantation, all the operations?

All me.

And I adored it.

The Heights was *very* important to me, so being able to create something that impacted the community in such a positive way really made all the bullshit fade to background noise. I couldn't bring myself to give a fuck about what was happening in my personal life when my daily customer experience check told the story of an elder getting consistent transportation to her sewing club thanks to a teen who needed funds for their college applications and graduation expenses. Or the new mom who was thriving thanks to a weekly meal delivery from a private chef who was trying to get her business off the ground. And *so* many other stories.

Yes, a nominal fee was exchanged, but it was still neighbor helping neighbor and I was glad to facilitate.

The few hours I had to run through my administrative tasks flew by in a blur of refills and short –welcomed – interruptions from people I knew. I hated to break when I did, but I had to be available for my appointment time for the movers.

Not something I could miss.

Which made my decision to leave thirty minutes before, even though it was only a ten minute walk feel even wiser when I ran into Winnie, who was coming in as I was leaving.

"Ames – you haven't been to KANAOS class in like two weeks – what's going on?" she asked, greeting me with a hug, and stepping outside with me so we weren't blocking the door.

I returned her hug, but frowned at her words. "What is… what class did you say? Is that an acronym?"

She grinned. "It is – I'm workshopping the name," she explained. "It's the usual cardio kickboxing, but I want to promote it as *kick a nigga ass or something*," she said, with a flourish of her hands like she was visualizing it on a billboard.

"Kick a—Winnie, please," I giggled, and she shrugged.

"What?!" she asked, that grin getting even bigger. "Tell me I'm not on to something. Imagine it, you've been victimized physically or emotionally or hell – knowing some of these motherfuckers, *spiritually*, and you decide to get stronger, get some movement in, you know? You go looking for classes, you run across the acronym, and you wonder, *what's that*. Then you read the description, which includes the explanation of the acronym...," she said, still painting the picture. "Tell me what your reaction would be!"

I laughed. "This is insane... *but...* I think that's the class."

"Boom," Winnie nodded. "See? Jonathan thinks I'm bugging, but *I* think it's going to be a hit."

"You know Jonathan likes to keep it cute, so I understand him, but... I kinda like it. Keep talking to people about it, get some more feedback."

"Bet – but uh... my question still stands, friend. Where you been?"

"Well last week I just had a meeting, so I couldn't make it."

She squinted at me. "And... this week?"

"You already know what happened this week."

"Yeah," she sucked her teeth. "I'm saying – that shit is a perfect reason come kickbox, duh."

"I know," I laughed. "I just... I've been in a weird place."

"I get. You want me to kick that nigga ass or something?"

"Winnie!"

"What?" she shrugged. "I want the record to show that I *never* like him. For you specifically *or* otherwise. Like never, ever, at all."

"I'm aware," I nodded.

She had never, ever, at all, been quiet about it either, even to his face. In fairness though, her reasoning had never been like... *break up with him sis* type reasons.

She thought he was corny.

And physically weak.

And she didn't like his face.

And he didn't drink enough water for her liking.

Really random – and admittedly funny – stuff that I probably should've taken a little more seriously, considering how it all worked out.

"Okay, so like… do you need me to handle that?"

"No," I assured her. "There's nothing to handle. Just… two people it didn't work out between. Nothing more."

She twisted her lips like she was considering my words for a moment before she nodded. "Okay but if you change your mind – I've got a two piece for his ass I've *been* waiting to drop off."

"I'm not going to change my mind."

"Fine," she rolled her eyes. "I'll see you in class next week then, right?"

"I… yes. You will," I agreed before we parted ways. She was on a break between the fitness classes she hosted at the gym she owned with her boyfriend, and I had an appointment time to make.

Because of the time spent talking with Winnie, I had to put a little pep in my step to make it back with a little lead time before the movers arrived. Summer was in *full* effect, so by the time I made it to the building, I was a sweaty mess, debating on if I had time for a quick shower.

Which… actually wouldn't make sense, since I would just sweat through my clothes even more in the process of getting my stuff moved in.

Thank goodness for aluminum-laden deodorant I guess.

A thought occurred to me as I stored my few belongings out of the way on the kitchen counter, so I pulled my phone out to open the Proxy app for a new transaction.

Snacks and water.

Yeah, I had the few items I'd packed for my personal fulfilment, but I was sure the movers would appreciate cold drinks and a sandwich platter. With that order placed, I went back downstairs to navigate the truck to a more accessible, albeit temporary space.

And then I waited.

And... waited.

It was normal enough for the time to have five or ten minutes of wiggle room, but once that time had passed with no communication, that's when I got a little concerned.

I grabbed my phone, intending to check my appointment one more time, even though I knew I had the right date and time, and had gotten the confirmation and all.

Well... I *tried* to check it.

What actually happened was that I discovered my phone screen was frozen – a stupid glitch that been happening since I finally stopped postponing the last hardware update a few days ago.

Shit.

As soon as I restarted and unlocked it, the device started pinging with notifications.

A *you definitely fucked something up* amount of notifications.

"No," I groaned, already pouting as I read through the notifications letting me know the movers were arriving.

Had arrived.

Were waiting.

Would wait five more minutes.

Were giving me another five minutes as a courtesy.

Regrettably had to go.

I was still charged the full rate, plus the tip, because I always checked that box. And I couldn't even be *too* mad, because the movers had showed up.

On the right date.

At the appointed time.

At the agreed-upon location.

The townhouse I was supposed to be moving into.

Not this building.

I...

Okay.

Okay.

I tossed the phone onto the dashboard.

Closed my eyes.

Clenched my fists.

And... fuck it, I screamed.

And... I felt the tiniest bit better.

Until I opened my eyes, and locked gazes with my neighbor, who was standing on the sidewalk in front of the truck.

If his expression was any indication... I looked exactly as crazy as I felt.

Maybe crazier.

And then his face cracked into a laugh.

"No! *No!*" I declared, turning the ignition off and opening the door to climb down. "You do *not* get to laugh at me!"

He raised an eyebrow. "That's wild, considering that I'm *definitely* laughing right now."

"Nothing is funny!"

"You sitting alone in a moving truck screaming bloody murder is objectively funny as hell," he countered. "Are you cool?"

"No, I'm not fucking cool. *Clearly* I am not cool. I have not *been* cool. Are *you* cool?!"

"Breezy, actually," he grinned. "What's going on though? Seriously."

"Seriously?"

"Yes," he nodded. "This is a nice, peaceful neighborhood, and you're killing the vibe."

My mouth dropped. "*I'm* killing the vibe? *I'm kil*—you know what... no. No, I do not need your help."

"You *clearly* need help. Like... this a textbook case of someone needing help. Maybe on a clinical level."

"Oh is it clear? Really?" I sucked my teeth, turning back to the truck as he called behind me—

"In Eight-K-Ultra-High-Definition Sweetheart."

I couldn't keep the snarl off my face as I turned. "Sweetheart?! Who the fuck even are you?!"

"Calvin Cross," he answered, extending a hand in my direction with a stupid grin.

It took *all* my self control not to slap it away, opting instead to simply ignore it as I crossed my arms. "Is that supposed to mean something to me?"

A look of surprise moved over his face as he pulled his hand back. "Oh. You've never watched—never mind. Look – like I said, you clearly need help. Whassup, your movers bailed on you or something?"

"Definitely something," I muttered under my breath, looking back at the truck as if... hell, I don't even know.

I was still in disbelief that I'd dropped the ball in such a manner.

"Ay – I've got other shit I could be doing right now," Calvin spoke up again, immediately inciting a raised eyebrow as I returned my gaze in his direction. "I'm

27

telling you I can give you a hand, but that offer expires in five... four—"

A countdown?

Is this nigga giving me a *countdown?*

"Three..."

He *is* giving me a countdown.

"Two..."

This is some bullshit.

"O—"

"Fine!" I cut in. "You can help me."

His face wrinkled into a scowl. "Uh... thanks for the opportunity?"

"You're welcome."

"You're mean as fuck," he chuckled, shaking his head as he walked around to the back of the truck. "Open it up, let me see what we're dealing with."

For a moment, I could even think about the instruction – I was caught up on the accusation – *mean.*

Was I being mean?

And if *yes,* enough for *mean as fuck* to be accurate?

Damn.

Okay.

I needed to chill.

None of this is his fault.

He's trying to help you.

Don't be a bitch.

"It's not a ton of stuff," I explained as I unlocked and unlatched the roll-up door. "I tend towards minimalism anyway, and even half of *that* is in storage from moving in with Hun—with my ex," I corrected.

"That's tough – you moved in with a ni—well, let me not assume."

My eyebrows shot up. "Not assume what?"

"That your ex was a nigga," he shrugged. "You kinda give *those* vibes."

"Excuse me?!"

"Not in a bad way," he continued, peeking into the truck. "Like you *only* fuck with white boys. In you'll fuck with anybody kinda way."

My frown deepened. "You realize that's *more* offensive, right?"

"Shit – I'm not articulating myself well," he chuckled. "You're the equal opportunity type."

"An equal opportunity *whore*?" I questioned, propping hands on my hips.

"No judgement here." He hit me with a dazzling grin, then looked back to my stuff. "This shouldn't take that long sweetheart."

"*Stop* calling me that."

"My bad – what do you prefer? Babe? Shorty? Ma'am?"

I rolled my eyes. "Amelia is just fine."

"Cool – let's get to it, Amy."

Who the fuck is Amy was the question I successfully kept in my brain, off my lips. It was clear at this point that he was hellbent on wrecking my already flayed nerves, and I was not trying to give him any more encouragement.

We did, indeed, get to it.

Me struggling with plastic totes I'd overpacked in effort to use as few as I possibly could, him carrying them two at a time like they were nothing. We worked together on the furniture, including the deceptively heavy mattress box I undid as soon as we had it in the room.

It would take hours and hours to get to proper size, and I wanted that process starting ASAP.

We were on the last trip up the elevator, just waiting for the doors to close when they suddenly reversed course, letting another resident onto the elevator.

Immediately, I wanted to sink through the floor.

Hunter saw me first – I watched the surprise, then confusion register on his face before he noticed Calvin, whose presence brought a different, unfamiliar something to his expression. I quickly shifted my gaze away, sinking back deeper into the elevator – unfortunately closer to Calvin.

Who, for some inexplicable reason... wrapped his arm around my neck.

Pulled me into him.

Lord it felt good.

I forced myself not to close my eyes, giving myself – completely inappropriately – over to the feeling of being touched by someone who wasn't Hunter.

A practical stranger, but still.

"You good sweetheart?" Calvin asked, lips brushing my forehead to really sell... whatever story he was painting right now.

I... was too shocked to do anything but nod.

He looked right at Hunter, who'd stepped into the elevator now, and said, "What's good, man? What floor you on?"

Six.

"Uhh... six," Hunter answered, and Calvin nodded before he pressed it.

I didn't dare look at his face, but his shoes were still facing us as the door closed.

Slow as hell.

"Just moving in?" Hunter asked, and Calvin was quick with the answer.

"Nah, I been here for a while, on and off – she is, though. Couldn't let her bring all this in by herself with the week she's had, you know?" Calvin replied, giving me a little squeeze before he took the box I was holding and stacked it with the ones he'd sat down.

Oh my God.

"Is that right?"

I could feel Hunter's eyes on me, feel the questions radiating.

Thank the *lord* we were on two.

Those doors couldn't open soon enough.

I shot past him without looking, not caring how crazy I likely appeared. Behind me, Calvin was moseying off the elevator, boxes stacked three high.

"Hope to see you back on the court," Hunter called after him, and Calvin gave him a head raise in return for whatever the fuck that meant, and then... the elevator chimed and moved on.

I got my door unlocked and held it open for Calvin to put my boxes down, and as soon as he had, he looked at me with a grin.

"So... who was that?"

4 /
amelia

"Now you know good and goddamn well who that was!" spilled from my lips before I could help it – *not* that I was trying to help it.

I was holding on to sanity by the frayed, tattered edges right now, and didn't have the bandwidth for much of anything else.

Calvin grinned harder.

Okay... I had the bandwidth for *nothing* else, because – "okay, thanks for your help, but I need you to immediately get outta my face, cause what's funny, huh?"

"I didn't say anything was funny!" he claimed, tossing up his hands.

Still grinning.

"I'm just a jovial kinda guy, what's wrong with that?"

"Right now? Everything. *Good. Damn. Bye.*"

I stomped back to my front door, swinging it open to find Hunter at my door, *looking stupid*, hand poised to knock.

"What do you want?" I asked, not bothering to tuck away any of my annoyance.

Ever-so-slightly, his head reared back, surprised by

33

my energy. "Uh… I just wanted to ask if we could talk for a second?"

I shot a glare into the apartment at Calvin, whose attention was on the food I'd put out for the movers, then looked back to Hunter. On a deep sigh, I stepped out and closed the door, crossing my arms.

"What?"

Again, he did that little pull-back thing, like he was just so appalled by my attitude – which, for the record, was *really* only making my attitude *worse.*

"Damn, Amelia – it's gotta be hostile?"

I shrugged. "Gotta? No. Is? Kinda. It hasn't exactly been a great week for me."

"I get that," he nodded. "But… you're the one who didn't even want to talk. You weren't even trying to give me a chance to explain myself."

I sucked my teeth. "What was there to explain? *I'm not sure about this anymore* is a very clear statement."

"It's a normal thing to feel!" he argued. "Checking in with yourself or some shit, I don't know!"

My eyes narrowed. "Normal? Yes. A sign to fucking break up? *Also yes.*"

"Not necessarily!" Hunter scoffed. "You're gonna stand here and tell me you never wondered if we were right for each other or not?"

"Of course I did, because I'm not some desperate weirdo wanting a relationship at all cost. But the answer was always *yes*. Do I love him? Do I trust him? Can I see myself as his wife? Forever? Kids? *Yes. Yes. Yes. Yes. Yes!*" I shot at him, stepping a little closer every time. "But for *you*, damn near three years in, *you're not sure about this anymore!*"

"Which is why I asked you to move in!" he argued. "I

34

thought maybe we were just too busy, not seeing each other enough anymore. You were so busy getting Proxy off the ground, so I thought it would bring us closer, remind us what it was... you know?"

"Are you... are you *kidding me*?!" I hissed. "You weren't sure... *before* you asked me to uproot my life to move into *your*.... Hunter..."

He took a step back, hands up. "Whoa... why did you just say my name like that?"

"Who... the fuck... asks somebody... they *aren't sure* about... to *move in with them*?!"

"I explained!"

"And now I'm waiting for you to say some shit that actually makes sense!" I shot back, quickly swiping away the sudden stream of tears that decided to show up.

The *last* thing I wanted was for his ass to see me crying over him.

"Amelia... just... come up to the apartment, let's sit down and talk through—"

"There is not a single thing for us to talk through!" I told him, batting away the "comforting" hand he'd tried to place on my shoulder. "You will not waste another moment of my time."

He scoffed, stepping away as his face wrinkled in disdain. "Yeah – you're real strict about that, huh?"

"What the *fuck* is that supposed to mean?"

"I see you haven't wasted any time finding somebody else to be up under," he snapped, and my eyes narrowed in absolute confusion until his gaze shifted to my door.

Goddamn Calvin.

"You don't even know what you're talking about," I said, and he shrugged.

"I know what I saw – you on some athlete's arm,

35

which is *exactly* the shit… you know what… nevermind," he shook his head. "If this is what it is… fuck it I guess. I'll tell momma not to ask about you anymore."

I gasped. "You'd *better not*, Mrs. Linda can ask about me anytime she wants!"

He just stared at me for a few seconds before the tension in his shoulders slumped. "Yeah. I would never tell her not to ask about you. She loves you."

"And I love her," I replied.

And you.

Loved you.

"How is Maggie?" he asked, almost bringing the slightest smile to my face.

"She's good. She's going to bring you cucumbers from her vines next time she comes up."

His eyebrows went up. "Does she know we…"

"She knows."

"And she's still bringing them for me?"

"She's gotta give that shit to somebody – her words," I said.

There was quiet for a moment, and then, "Are you going to give them to me when she brings them?"

"I'll leave them at your door."

Eyebrows back up. "Intact, or…?"

"I haven't decided yet," I shrugged. "And… I don't want to talk to you right now, so can this be… done?"

"This conversation, or… us?"

I laughed.

To not burst into tears, even though it was a *really* fine line.

"Both," I replied. "I'm telling you – we're done."

Hunter's jaw went tense, and he blinked a few times before he nodded. "I guess that's it then."

"I guess so."

He opened his mouth like he had one more thing to say... then changed his mind, or thought better of it, something. Whatever it was... he didn't say anything else, just headed to the elevator.

Head down, shoulders slumped, looking pitiful.

As if this wasn't *his* fault.

Instead of watching his sad performance, I went aside, closing and locking the door behind me.

I... kinda wanted to scream again.

Instead... I cried.

The tears I'd been doing my damndest to hold back in front of Hunter all broke free, and before I knew it I was full-blown sobbing. I dropped to a seat on the floor, hugging my legs, head resting on my knees as I cried myself into a headache.

And then... the feeling in the room shifted.

My head popped up, looking around for the culprit... landing on Calvin.

Looking stupid.

"Oh *God*," I groaned, and then... fuck it, cried harder, because quite literally, *what the fuck was my life.*

A joke, Ames.

"*Shit*," I heard him mutter, and my neck snapped up, glaring at him through my tears.

"Yeah, no kidding," I sobbed, scrubbing hands over my wet face. "Not exactly my proudest moment here."

He nodded. "This is a lot," he said, coming to crouch beside me, so close his clean, woody scent filled my nose. "What that nigga say to you? You want me to fuck him up? I don't mind, seriously. I *been* needing to get some aggression out."

I shook my head, taking a deep breath to try to calm myself. "No. I don't want that."

"Yeah, he probably ain't pissed you off enough yet. Anything else I can do?"

"No." I wiped my eyes. "I'm good," I declared, pulling myself to a stand.

"Aiight. Well, I found your pink tool set and put the bed frame together for you while you were talking to ol' boy."

"Really? Wow," I muttered. "Thank you – that thing has driven me nuts every time I've had to deal with it."

"It was nothing. I'm good at beds."

My face went hot, and I frowned. "Wait... what did you just say?"

He smirked. "I said I'm good *at* beds – like, building them. But what you thought I said..." he smirked, giving me slow once-over that made my face hot. "That is also true. Can I take this?" he asked, pointing to the last of the food for the movers.

"Yeah," I sighed. "Knock yourself out."

"Thanks," he said, closing the container, preparing to scoop it up before he stopped and looked at me. "Aye... Do you want to...?"

I raised an eyebrow. "Do I want to... *what*?" I asked, confused.

He shrugged. "You know... try out that bed frame?"

"Nigga... are you trying to fuck me?!" I asked, scandalized by the question *and* the fact that my thighs clenched at the prospect.

Very whorish, Amelia.

Equal Oppurtunity.

"I'm offering!" he defended. "You look good, I look good. You're sad – I'm willing to be used as a distraction

38

from that. I'm just trying to be a good neighbor! I'm very, *very* good at it."

"You have done enough – *more than*," I snapped. "Thank you. You can go."

He chuckled. "Fair enough. I can still take this, right?"

"Take them sandwiches and get the fuck on!" I hissed.

"You don't have to yell, damn," he said, tucking the tray under his arm, and grabbing a few water bottles too. "Can you get the door for me?"

I blew out a sigh. "Yes. Come on," I said, and started for it *immediately*.

Cause… *what the actual fuck.*

I flung my door open for him, directing him out. He didn't linger inside, but in the hall, he did hit me with another grin. "If you change your mind… that second offer stands too."

I rolled my eyes. "I'll keep it under consideration."

"You think you could help with my do—"

I closed my damn door.

Before I said something stupid.

Did something stupid.

Like fucking that man.

It was tempting.

Quite.

For myriad reasons.

Distraction, as he'd mentioned.

Loneliness.

Sadness.

Spite.

And if I was even the tiniest bit more inclined toward the *Equal Opportunity Whoredom* we'd bandied about, I just might be opening my door to catch him before he got inside.

As it stood… there was too much happening in my head now, all on top of the fact that I was supposed to be getting back into work for the afternoon.

Which, the chances of now were pretty low.

Like, *zero* low.

Instead, I went to my bedroom to inspect Calvin's job putting together the bedframe – it was more sturdy than I'd ever been able to get it, even with Hunter's help, actually. Despite the mattress not being fully inflated yet, I dragged it to the bed, put fresh sheets on it, and curled up in the covers.

Maybe my luck at life would be better tomorrow.

5 /
calvin

"DAMN, you really gone leave that *horse* on one leg, ain't it?!"

I closed my eyes – partially to keep the sweat out, partially to take a moment to not curse Arthur's ass out.

I hadn't asked for spectators – I *never* did – and yet, somehow, he found himself out here offering commentary on my daily drills.

At this point, I chose to think of his bullshit as part of the training – hecklers never shut the fuck up either.

I used the least-soaked hem of my shirt to make a marginal difference in the sweat pouring down my forehead into my eyes, and then lined up my shot. I didn't let myself overthink it, just sent it gliding off my fingertips, through the hoop.

"There it is!" Arthur whooped from the concrete bench where he'd made himself – too – comfortable. "Keep that up they might take you back!"

My steps faltered as I headed for my rebound, stopping to shoot him a look I *hoped* would let him know I wasn't trying to be on that this morning.

At all.

41

I'd tuned out a lot, focusing on the beat in my headphones instead of his amateur commentating, but my absence from my team was still a little too much of a sore subject.

One moment.

One little loss of control.

And now my whole life was in lmbo.

As I bent to grab the ball, Arthur's voice rang out again, "Don't pull nothing out there – you getting up in age, and you'll find out the recovery is slower than it used to be."

"*Nigga*," I muttered under my breath, shaking my head as I stood. "What's the problem, man?" I asked, heading in his direction. "You ain't even said good morning, just straight to some bullshit."

Instead of contrition, I got laughter. "I forgot you like to fight. Don't come over here thinking I ain't got nothing for you though, youngin."

"You *just* said I was *getting up in age*," I countered, chuckling.

"For your profession," he clarified. "By the time you get back, them young cats gone be running circles around *Mr. Crossover*."

I scoffed. "The only time anybody getting one up on me is their *wildest* dreams, don't even play with me like that."

He tugged at the brim of his *Arthur's Tree Service* hat and nodded. "Confidence still intact, okay."

"Where else would it be?" I questioned, and he tossed his hands up.

"It was supposed to be a compliment."

"Felt like a jab."

"A jab would be reminding you that you still need an

S and an E," he cackled. "All that confidence, missing wide open shots. What would Coach Lewis have to say about *that*?"

"Man *fu*—" I groaned, and shut my damn mouth.

Nobody out here was reporting anything back, but still – it was better to not get comfortable letting how I really felt about *that* motherfucker come so freely off my lips.

But.

Fuck Coach Lewis.

While Arthur laughed, I jogged back to my mark.

Lined up my shot.

Made it.

Rebounded.

Made the other.

As easily as I really should've made the rest.

In my defense, I was at the end of a long conditioning session – the only reason I was outside in this heat anyway. A few miles through the neighborhood, some sprints on the court, pushups, all that.

Actual shooting practice was later.

Weights another day.

Everything to keep myself in a state that wouldn't discount me from stepping back into a role I never should've been pushed out of... but those were musings for another day.

Today, right now, I had a perfect vantage point of Amelia descending the front steps, pretty thighs on full display. She was wearing an oversized crew neck that covered all except a little peek of her shoulder and the very bottoms of bright yellow shorts that molded to her thighs and popped against her smooth, rich dark brown skin. Yoga mat tucked under her arm.

Arthur let out a low whistle. "You wouldn't even know what to do with that, boy, I don't know why you even bothering to look."

"Nah," I scoffed. "I know *exactly* what I'd do – *not* tell your ass shit, for sure," I muttered, leaving the ball to head to the sidewalk as she approached it. "Good morning, neighbor."

"Good morning," she returned my greeting with a smile – *pretty ass smile* – that immediately dropped from her face when I extended my arms in her direction. "Oh! I… uh… you're actually *really* sweaty and I—"

"Sweat is natural, and you're about to work out anyway, right? I see the yoga mat. Come on and get in here," I teased, knowing I wasn't *actually* about to touch her, even as I moved closer.

She gagged, though.

Like… *bad*.

"Oh, shit – I'm fucking with you," I explained, backing up as she clutched her stomach and nodded.

"Did you cut onions this morning or something?"

"*What*?!" I asked – appalled, quite frankly – at what she was insinuating. I put my nose to my arm as Arthur cackled in the background.

"She said you smell like one of them bougie salads!"

"Nigga shut up!" I yelled, then turned back to her. "Ay – whatever you smelling, it's not—*Oh*."

I cut off my defense mid-sentence as I clocked the self-satisfied smirk on her pretty face.

"You got jokes this morning, huh?" I asked, crossing my arms.

"Just a little. You *are* disgustingly sweaty right now though, please stay back."

I grinned, and took a step closer. "What, you sweat-phobic or something? Is there a word for that?"

"*Backthefuckup* is the word for it," she said, putting up a hand. "But no – I'm not *sweat-phobic*, it's just... a bodily fluid."

"You don't like swapping bodily fluids?"

Her eyes narrowed. "Outside a very, *very* limited set of circumstances, no."

"Okay, tell me the circumstances," I shrugged. "We can arrange that shit. Starting *now*."

"Boy!" she laughed. "Tell me – do women usually respond favorably to this kind of blatant propositioning?"

"Looking like I do? Yeah," I laughed. "They love the candor, the interest is reciprocated... the inevitable is obvious..."

Her eyebrows shot up. "The inevitable is obvious?"

"That's what I said."

"Like... right now?"

I shrugged. "I'd say so."

Her gaze locked onto mine, determined. "You know I'm *never* going to fuck you, specifically because of this conversation, right?"

"I've come to a very different conclusion from it."

She scoffed. "Yeah... *never*."

"Why would you deny yourself the pleasure of my dick?"

"*Wow*," she laughed. "You are *so* full of yourself."

"And you could be full of me too, but you playing around."

"Can you leave me alone?" she asked, then bit down on her lip – trying her *damndest* not to smile before she added a "*please*?"

I smirked.

45

Stepped closer – *right* on the line of probably too close – meeting her gaze as I told her in a low tone, *"Only because you said please."*

She gulped a little.

I saw it.

I *heard* it.

Got her.

"Goodbye, Calvin."

I straightened to full height to wave. "Bye Li-Li."

She'd already started moving down the sidewalk, but looked back with a frown. "Li-Li? Don't do that," she laughed, then crossed the street.

Ass swaying in little peeks under the hem of her sweatshirt.

She is bad as fuck, man.

"That box-head nigga from upstairs gone fuck you up about that girl," Arthur cackled, from *way* closer than he'd been when I stopped paying attention to him. "You know that's his lady, right?"

I sucked my teeth. "Nah, he fumbled her."

"They ain't done – they was together too long – I'm telling you," Arthur warned. "And that boy got money."

My face dropped into a frown as I turned to grab my ball. "So? I got money too."

"The fuck you hanging around here for then?" he countered, and I sighed.

"Because this is home? It's low-key, nobody bothers me for autographs and shit."

"Cause don't nobody know who you are."

"They know who I am, be serious."

"She don't."

Damn.

Okay.

He had me on that one.

"Don't you have a list of maintenance requests you should be handling right now instead of bothering me?" I asked.

"I ain't on the clock yet."

"But you're punched all the way in on *my* business? That's craaaazy," I said, heading into the side door of the building.

With him *right* behind me.

"Somebody has to look in on you – make sure you're not getting too comfortable."

"What does *that* mean?" I asked, frowning as I stopped at the door to the stairs.

He shrugged. "I've seen a lot of cat get a little too comfortable sitting out. Start doing other shit – never make it back to the game. Look at Ambrose McNeil."

"From the Kings?" I asked. "He came back from his injury, had a great season…"

"Yeah, and then he got shot behind somebody else's woman," Arthur cackled and I rolled my eyes. "He ain't seeing the field again – those some nice ass watches he be selling though."

"Are you implying the wack ass dude from upstairs is going to *shoot me* for flirting with my neighbor?"

"I'm just saying it's a possibility – and you know damn well flirting ain't all you trying to do."

I chuckled. "It's all I'll ever discuss with your gossiping ass," I told him, then pulled the door open for the stairs.

I took them two at a time, ready to get out of my sweaty clothes and into the shower. Now that I wasn't in the moment, the fatigue of my workout was starting to register in my limbs.

I checked my phone for anything emergent, then went about my usual routine – quick protein shake, shower, and then back to my phone.

I was *not* comfortable, not at all.

I was essentially unemployed, and though bills weren't a concern due to savvy planning and smart savings, my future?

I was *very* fucking concerned.

Basketball was my job – my *life*.

I wasn't on any superstar status shit like Kevion or Thierry – *neither* of them could walk around the Heights or Blackwood like a regular person, while I still had that freedom.

I hadn't had my "breakout" season yet.

I'd been, I believed, on the verge.

But then bullshit came knocking, and my stupid ass answered the door.

Now, instead of working out in the Brawler team facilities... I was running drills on cracked concrete in an empty lot.

I wasn't defeated, though.

Benched, maybe.

I was *not* comfortable, but I was confident – I had more wins coming.

And one of them had just moved in next door.

6 /
amelia

I DID *NOT* LIKE UNPACKING.

Dare I say – I hated it.

Did I know I hated it?

No.

But it was the only logical conclusion for why, instead of unpacking, I was taking down box braids that I could've easily gotten another two weeks out of.

A month with the right headbands and scarves.

As soon as the last one came out, I was hit with an immediate sense of regret – I loved my natural hair, real bad, but I'd just added at least twenty minutes to my daily morning routine by having it out.

Not to mention the whole wash-day ritual I was about to have to go through.

And all for what reason?

To avoid unpacking them fucking boxes.

Excellent decision-making, Ames.

In the mirror, I surveyed my hairline, making sure it was still intact after a hellish soft-loc experience a few years back. Once I was satisfied that I hadn't destroyed any follicles this time around, I started gathering my

49

supplies to do a real detangle before I put my head under the water.

A process interrupted by a knock at the door.

Immediately, I frowned – I wasn't expecting anyone, and my friends and I weren't "pop up" kinda people. My next thought was that maybe it was Hunter, which set off a confusing mix of emotions – the exact thing I'd been trying to avoid by zoning out on social media while I did the braid takedown.

Two weeks out of a long-term relationship, I was still, in fact... sad.

Hell, two weeks was pushing it – eleven days.

It came and went in waves of course, and life moved on, but the possibility of running into him not just out and about in the neighborhood but *in the damn building*?

Made me want to stay cloistered in the safety (emotional, and relative) of my apartment.

Or not even go home.

I hated the feeling, but... it was where life had landed me, for now. A repeated knock on the door reminded me this wasn't the time for musings – and also let me know it was *not* Hunter at the door.

Whoever was at the door was currently recreating the Clipse *Grindin'* beat.

Definitely Calvin type behavior.

Luckily, my preliminary detangle had left me with hair that needing washing still, but was presentable enough to interact with the public. I took advantage of the peephole, frowning a bit at the unfamiliar face.

I recognized the oversized *Proxy* delivery tote in their hands, though.

"Can I help you?" I asked, opening the door even though I hadn't ordered anything.

I was met with a – very glittery – grin from the woman standing there, who gave me a onceover as she nodded.

"Whassup – I'm Jeanie," she said, and I raised an eyebrow.

"Okay... nice to meet you Jeanie... I'm Amelia."

"Oh I assure you, the pleasure is mine," she told me, licking her lips.

Is she serious?

"Is that a delivery?" I asked, trying to redirect Jeanie and her grill and tatted arms.

She looked down at the bag like she'd forgotten it was there, and nodded. "Oh – yeah," she said, maneuvering the top of the tote open to remove a greasy cardboard box and a plastic container of salad.

Why did I accept the food into my hands?

Reflex, confusion, stupidity, some mixture of all of the above.

Whatever it was, I immediately regretted it, because... grease.

And it literally *smelled* like heartburn.

"So Amelia... what you getting into tonight?" Jeanie asked. "You busy or something?"

"Why?" I asked, already knowing what was happening, but wanting to hear it.

For research.

She grinned – there were dimples! – doing that lip bite thing again before she answered. "I'm saying... you heard of Christina Aguilera, right? That song—"

"Girl!" I cut her off, choking back a laugh. "Are you not mid-delivery right now?"

"I ain't worried about that – my backpack is downstairs in my car. You got your food, them other folks can wait for me to make some wishes come true, you know what I'm saying?"

I scoffed. "I know exactly what you're saying – you *really* shouldn't be saying it to me."

Her eyebrows went up. "Oh my bad, you not with the rainbow?"

"That is quite literally not at all the point," I answered. "You should not be propositioning me while providing a service – and not even doing it well."

"You saying I don't have motion?"

"I'm saying I didn't order this," I explained, holding up the box that was making a mess of my hands. "It's clearly been in this box a long time – longer than it should. And you had the salad in the hot bag with it, so that's not even edible anymore." I peeked at the ticket taped to the salad container. "This order was placed two hours ago. The pickup time was an hour and a half ago. Bella's is literally five minutes from here. What were you doing?"

Jeanie shrugged. "I had other orders, my bad."

"There's no way this doesn't mess with your rating in the app."

Her eyes went wide. "You gone one-star me over a little flirting? That's cold, pretty girl. It's also giving a little 'phobic… a little *anti* if you know what I mean."

"I know you need to be *so* for real right now," I countered, trying to hand her the food back. "I can't rate you, because it's not my order, first of all. Second, I was referencing you taking your sweet time to deliver food that cannot be eaten."

She sucked her teeth. "Man, whatever – I got my girl waiting in the car, and other orders. I don't have time for this."

"You were offering to go get your backpack while you have somebody waiting in the car for you? Get the fuck on somewhere, and take this shit with you," I said, not even trying to keep it even slightly professional anymore.

"What the fuck am I gonna do with that?" she said, heading down the hall. "I'll just mark it delivered in the app."

"That's a lie!" I called after her, and she turned to me with that glittery grin.

"What can *you* do about it?" she shrugged. "You can't rate me, and Calvin from the second floor didn't have enough sense to put his apartment number, so... fuck it. Y'all have a good night."

And then she was gone, taking the stairs instead of waiting on the elevator.

Leaving me standing in the hall with calzone grease dripping on the floor.

"What can *I* do about it?" I asked myself out loud. "She said *what can you do about it* like I can't fucking do something about it," I muttered, stepping back into my apartment and closing the door. "I'ma show you what I can fucking do about it."

Inside, I started to drop the food into the trash, then opted for the counter instead. I scrubbed my hands – and then cussed Jeanie's ass out a little more as I cleaned up the trail of grease on the floor.

Once that was done, I went for my computer, navigating to the *Proxy* system that contained our database of "partners" – the people who provided service to others in whatever capacity.

For now, I was looking for the food delivery drivers.

I was able to find the profile easily – there was more than one "Jeanie" in various spellings, but the ratings and

53

reviews made it simple to pick out the right one. She was consistently late, often inappropriate, and the person pictured on the profile was *not* actually her, which was a security violation I made a note to speak to that team about. The only thing keeping her account from being restricted due to low-performance was the occasionally five-stars that I suspected were coming from women who'd waited on the backpack.

"VERY satisfactory delivery, would rate ten stars if I could. Attentive and focused. Hands-on service. Very communicative. Timely. Highly recommend if you need a personal touch."

On a fucking bbq plate dropoff?

There was no damn way.

For now, I simply flagged the account to have a discussion with the right people, instead of restricting it, or simply shutting her down like I wanted. Because I'd had a direct – contentious – interaction with her, there would be a need to speak with legal, blah, blah, blah.

It was all so annoying.

Especially since she'd introduced two new considerations - *how* were people getting around the identity verification, and at least equally concerning, *were folks slinging dick on my app?!*

Wait, correction.

Were folks slinging strap on my app?!

This was the kind of thing Hunter would've complained about – me getting derailed from what I was doing in "non Proxy" time, which was usually giving him my attention, to do "Proxy" things.

Yet, when *he* was busy with work stuff, and I had to entertain myself during time that was supposed to be *ours*, it was fine.

Another red flag I never should've ignored.

My air conditioning kicked on, bringing a little hint of a "breeze" with it - a breeze that brought that nauseating scent of Calvin's misdelivered food wafting into my space. I immediately wrinkled my nose, trying to keep it at bay, to no avail.

I had to get it out of here, one way or another.

A glance at the time told me it was later than I'd even realized – certainly too late on a weekday to order something else. There was music coming from his apartment, but I'd come to understand that didn't mean anything – there was *always* music, even when he wasn't being obnoxious.

This was a time when I wished we'd exchanged numbers – I could just shoot him a text, or call. *Very* briefly I entertained the idea of grabbing it from his customer profile, or messaging him in the app, but that was a privacy violation I *definitely* didn't need to be getting involved in.

I was going to have to go knock on the door.

Shit.

I stuck the food in a *Proxy* bag I had from a delivery of my own, cleaned the grease off my counter, and then headed for the door. I was halfway out when I made a quick u-turn back to my bedroom to put a hoodie on over the lounge shorts and tank I'd been wearing.

I did *not* want to knock on that man's door looking like a booty call.

With a little more coverage on my side, I resumed my task of closing this loop I'd been pulled into, through no fault of my own.

I knocked… and didn't get an answer.

Knocked a little louder… no answer.

Knocked as hard as I dared… and still no answer.

55

Hm.

Probably sleeping, I told myself, then turned back for my own apartment. I'd just tell him about it when I saw him next, or maybe slip him a note.

Yeah.

I'd slip him a note.

I was already formulating it in my head as I opened my door – and then *his* door opened, finally.

And his dick stepped outside.

I mean… Calvin stepped out.

Dick first.

He was wearing boxers, sure.

But like… damn.

Why can't I look away?

Is it… hypnotizing me?!

Damn.

"Amelia… what's up?" he groggily asked, unaware of the commotion the protrusion in his boxers was causing in my head.

Heart.

Panties.

"Oh. Uh… you ordered food?" I asked, holding the bag up. "The driver came to my apartment instead – I think you didn't put the apartment number?"

He squinted at me, leaning in the doorway. Behind him, the apartment was dark and still, not even the flicker of a TV. Just his music.

He scrubbed a hand over his sleep-swollen face like he was still trying to shake it all off. "Damn," he muttered. "That was some hours ago."

"Yeah – the driver kinda took their time delivering it. I don't think it's really edible anymore. Sorry."

Calvin shrugged as he scratched his head, inadver-

56

tently giving shape to the flattened coils on his left. I could tell exactly what side he'd been sleeping on.

Hard.

"You didn't do shit," he muttered, taking the bag from me. "Thank you for letting me know. I would've been wondering what the hell happened."

For some reasons, my eyes followed the bag as his hand dropped to his side... which led my gaze straight back to his dick.

He didn't notice.

When I forced my gaze back to his face, he was still clearly halfway out of it, enough to make me step forward a little.

"Hey... uh... are you okay?" I asked, and he immediately focused on me, nodding.

"Yeah, sorry. Just... shit, I didn't mean to crash like that."

I nodded. "Yeah, then you wake up all confused, and still tired..."

"Exactly," he nodded. "And now I'm about to be up all night looking stupid."

I laughed. "Yeah... can unfortunately relate. Busy day?"

"I wish," he scoffed. "Just... workout, sit around. Work out some more, sit around. Living the dream," he said, words dripping with a kind of bitter sarcasm I'd *never* heard from him before. "Shit," he mumbled. "Uh... thank you again for letting me know what happened with this."

"Of course," I replied. "I kinda feel bad for waking you up."

"You can wake me up for anything, Sweetheart."

Ooh.

57

In that low, groggy, tone, that shit made my stomach flip.

"I told you to stop calling me that," I said, trying to deflect from my visceral reaction to him.

"My bad Li-Li."

"*Not that either!*" I insisted with a groan. "See? Nevermind about feeling bad."

He put a hand to his chest. "You're turning on me so easily in my vulnerable moment, damn."

"Vulnerable moment?" I asked, and he blinked a bit, like was processing his own words before he shook his head, shuttering whatever had been there the moment before.

"You don't see how exposed I am right now?" he asked, gesturing at his dick.

Deflecting.

I rolled my eyes. "I'm trying my hardest not to."

He grinned. "Why? You can look. We love attention."

"We?"

"Me and my dick. We could use some comfort."

"Is that so?" I laughed. "Well, I'm going to let the two of you get right to it. Y'all have fun," I said, taking a step back.

"Without you?" he asked as I opened my door.

I shrugged. "Uh… I'm there in spirit?"

Now why the fuck would you say that?

No, literally.

Why the fuck did I say that?

Calvin clearly thought the same, based on the surprise registered on his face, followed immediately by a downright *lusty* grin.

Shit!

I couldn't close that door fast enough.

7 /
amelia

CALVIN WAS ABOUT to leave his apartment.

After living here for two weeks, I'd already picked up the patterns in the thumps and bumps from next door, the music he typically played, and *very* loosely, the time of day.

I... was not sure that man had a job.

Which made it all the more difficult to avoid running into him, which was a fucked up thing to even have to do when I was already avoiding a *different* man from this building.

It was starting to give *prisoner in my own home* vibes, and I was *not* a fan.

Fuck it.

I was ready to go, so I was going.

Calvin opened his door at the *exact* same time I did.

I started to quickly dart back inside – and hell, I probably would've if he didn't spot me.

But he *did* spot me.

"Good morning, Sunshine," he greeted. "You get it – cause you're wearing yellow?"

I sighed, not cracking a smile. "Yes, Calvin. I get it. Good morning."

He scoffed. "Fine then – how about *Pissy?* I think it's more fitting."

My lips twitched then – I *wanted* to laugh, but couldn't have him thinking shit was sweet. "Hey – that's not necessary!" I scolded, following him down the hall.

"Neither is your attitude, but since that's what you're on this morning, let's match energy."

He stopped at the elevator to look me dead in the face, waiting on me to challenge that.

Which I *did*.

"I'm not being *pissy*," I replied. "I just... I didn't want to talk to you this morning, but there you were, and you just came straight out the gate with the charm, and it annoyed me, so I..."

"Decided to be pissy," he shrugged. "Just own it."

I let out a huff. "Fine. Maybe I *am* being pissy."

"Definitely. You even wore the uniform."

I rolled my eyes. "So if I'm nice to you, it's sunshine, if I'm mean, it's piss?"

"Yeah, exactly."

Both our heads turned as a loud *clang* came from the elevator, followed shortly by a long buzz that definitely didn't seem right.

Calvin let out an audible grunt, then turned for the stairs. After a moment, I was right behind him.

Whatever the elevator had going on this morning, I wasn't really trying to be part of it.

"So what did I do for your mood to turn pissy just because I spoke?" Calvin asked, taking the stairs two at a time on those long ass legs.

"Can we stop saying that word? It's starting to grate on me."

"What, pissy?" he asked, giving me a mischievous grin over his shoulder as we went through the door to the lobby instead of the side door that would take us out to the court – where I'd assumed he was going, for some reason.

He was dressed, but not like *dressed*.

Dressed to maybe hit the gym, with the accompanying bag slung over his shoulder.

I didn't ask.

Wouldn't ask, because, it wasn't my business.

Except… now we were at the street, walking together.

"You gonna answer the question?" he spoke up, pulling my attention from my internal musings.

"What question?"

"About why you don't wanna talk to me."

Oh.

That question.

"It's not personal," I explained. "Not really. I just… you make me feel very…"

"Hot? Sexy? Fine?"

"See?!" I laughed. "I'm trying to be serious, and your ass is… silly, and… distracting. And… I'm in this place where I don't know if it's healthy or wise to…"

"Have fun?"

"*Engage,*" I corrected. "I'm just… very uncalibrated right now. I just moved, just ended a relationship, just took my braids down, my luteal phase is right around the corner – it's just too fucking much. And then here you come, looking like you look, making me laugh and getting under my skin, and like I said… *distracting.*"

61

His smile dropped – not into a frown, just... focus. He was actually listening. "From the too-muchness?"

"Exactly," I nodded. "And I don't want to end up in some weird ass, toxic *thing* because I got caught up in a moment instead of actually processing."

"Fair enough. What does processing look like?"

"Uhh... feeling my feelings instead of running from them," I answered. "I remember talking about it with my therapist some years back – any time we have negative emotions, we want to rush past it, or push it behind something to avoid it, but that just prolongs it. I have to let myself be sad about the breakup. Mad about it. *Hurt.*"

"That apply to other stuff too? Just gotta sit in it and feel it?"

I nodded. "Yeah, I think so."

"How do you make sure you're not like... wallowing, though?" he asked as we approached a crosswalk. "What's the balance?"

"That is a great question I do not know the answer to," I laughed. "I wish I did."

"Yeah, me too," Calvin chuckled. "Sitting in it just feels so..."

"Bad?" I offered, and he nodded.

"Shit is draining."

"That's kinda the point though, right? To wring all the bullshit out, and then... replenish?"

"With what?"

I shrugged as we crossed the street. "I don't know – that depends on the person. Whatever makes you feel... full."

"Got it. So.. Family. Basketball. Flirting with my pretty ass new neighbor..."

"Damn – third on the priority list, huh?"

"There's room to move up in ranks."

I shook my head. "I don't think I want to even know what the promotion tract looks like there."

"Painless," he swore. "I mean… unless you're *into*—"

"Okay this is my stop," I spoke over him, laughing as I pointed to Urban Grind. "I need to get some work done."

He chuckled, shifting his bag up onto his shoulder a little more securely. "Yeah, me too. Headed to PT."

"Physical therapy?" I asked, confused. I'd *definitely* seen him in action on that basketball court beside our building. He was fast, confident, and often shirtless – a breathtaking example of what God was capable of creating to be quite frank. "Did you hurt yourself or something?"

"Old nagging injury," he explained, moving to cross the street alone. "No big deal, just keeping on top of it so I don't end up in a bad spot with it."

"Oh, gotcha. Well… good luck with that."

"And good luck with work," he said, with a parting wave.

I did *not* watch him cross the street.

I went inside.

And watched him travel the sidewalk from there instead.

Like a proper lady.

But then I was off that, and onto what I'd gotten up to do – work. I ordered my latte and pastry and then found myself a little spot where I could settle into my task list. Before I knew it, an hour had passed, and Shia was slipping into the other seat at the table I'd chosen, with her own coffee in hand.

"Morning," I greeted with a smile. "Thank you for making time."

She gave me a dry laugh in return. "Man, please. I didn't have a choice – that Jeanie chick is a lawsuit waiting to happen."

My eyes went wide, and I leaned in. "Nooo," I whispered. "Did you find more red flags?"

"Enough to lead a communist revolution."

"Don't tell me that," I whined, and Shia shook her head.

"I'm sorry to have to – look at this," she said, opening her laptop to turn the screen in my direction. "She's had two more complaints in the time since you flagged her. One was just late, but the other... the groceries didn't have bags. She just put the stuff on the doorstep, scattered, and a neighbors dog got into it and got sick."

I dropped my head into my hands. "We've terminated her account, right?"

"For the *third* time, yeah," Shia explained. "I've got the security team trying to figure out how the hell she keeps getting around the background checks."

"*Three* times?!"

"She's persistent, if nothing else. And well-reviewed at the none-delivery deliveries."

I frowned. "What does that mean?"

Shia smirked, clicking around a bit on her screen before she turned it to me again. "Read this new review."

"I'm scared."

"Just read it," she insisted, and I accepted the challenge, focusing on the words she'd directed my attention to.

My mouth fell open halfway through the second sentence.

"This reads like a damn erotica. I'm not grown enough for whatever this is," I said, pushing it away. "It's for sure not about groceries or take out."

"Oh, she's been taking something out for sure," Shia laughed.

"Flag that girl's license, social, birth certificate, diploma, library card, hell, her shoe size – whatever it takes to keep her off my shit before she gets me raided by VICE."

"Can you imagine the headline?"

"Yes, actually," I huffed. "*Lewd Lesbian Lunches Linked to Local Logistics.*"

"*Groceries Gone Wild,*" Shia countered, making me laugh even harder.

"Yeah, yeah – exactly the branding we've been going for!"

If it wasn't *actually* serious, the humor of it all could be a great marketing tactic – and Shia was the perfect person for it, as my Partner Relationship manager. She was the one who worked closely with the people providing the services on Proxy – making sure they were prepared and happy.

We joked a little longer about our Jeanie woes, but then someone else's laughter – familiar laughter – cut through the air, pulling my attention.

I immediately found the source.

Hunter.

I was tucked into a corner, out of direct view from most of the shop. I could see him, but he couldn't see me.

He was several tables away, leaning in close to the woman he was with. They'd pulled both chairs to the same side of the round table, obviously wanting to be

65

next to each other. Laughing, grinning, googly-eyes, all that.

Oh.

"Uh-oh," Shia muttered, clearly having followed my gaze, seeing the same thing I'd seen.

"No," I shook my head. "*Not* uh-oh. Just… a regular *oh*. Not a big deal."

She sucked her teeth. "Definitely a big deal – he's already grinning in another woman's face and it's barely been what… a damn fortnight?"

"In his defense, he saw me hugged up with my neighbor like a week ago."

Shia blinked. "Wait a minute… hugged up with a neighbor? Who?!"

"Nobody," I denied. "Or… not nobody, it just wasn't actually like that. He thought he was doing me a favor."

And shit… maybe he had.

Cause being posted up in Urban Grind with another woman – like he *wanted* it to be seen, to get back to me… Maybe I was overthinking it.

Or… maybe it was just a bitch move.

Either way, it was a poor use of my attention.

"So… about this Jeanie situation," I said, directing our meeting back on track. Shia gave me a look but didn't push it, shifting back to the matter at hand.

Thirty minutes later we had a plan in place – not just about Jeanie and her antics, but how to prevent future occurrences. When Shia decided she was going to head out, I opted to go too, hoping that having company would help me get out of the shop without interacting with Hunter.

Even though it was fine to leave your used dishes at

the tables, I never did, opting to drop them off at one of the little stations instead, to save the staff a bit of work.

It was just my luck that today, I was *almost* there, *almost* free… and then my mug slid off the saucer, rolling right into the dish station with a loud *clang* that brought all eyes to me.

No good deed goes unpunished.

My gaze immediately went to Hunter, who was, indeed, looking.

Hard.

Wondering.

I let my eyes narrow.

Yes, I see you.

Yes, I see her.

Yes, I care.

I looked away.

Slid my saucer into place where it was supposed to be, and went on about my business.

"You okay?" Shia asked as we left.

"Peachy."

8 /
amelia

I WENT to Winnie's class.

Unfortunately though, *Kick A Nigga Ass Or Something* was only a sufficient distraction while I was actively imagining Hunter's head as the target of my mimed punches.

Great workout though, and I was a little sad when it was over, entirely too soon.

Three sentiments that you *wanted* from a fitness class.

I made sure to share them with Winnie before I left – and made a note to tell Shia that one class member had crashed out mid-round on the ex she was pretending to fuck up.

Jeanie.

That girl was a damn menace.

I grabbed a togo plate from *Pot Liquor* on the walk home, tearing into the roasted chicken and greens as soon as I got through my front door, after smelling it the whole way. With my appetite sated and my energy zapped from class, all I had left to do was shower and go to bed, and hopefully wake up to a better day tomorrow.

I pulled out all my stuff for a *good* shower – limited

edition scents and the good exfoliating scrub, shave oils, all that. Instead of the overhead light, I set the mood with candles and music, stripped down, and got to work.

Everything else was so good that I wasn't even bothered when my music died halfway through – I finished taking my time scrubbing, shaving, smoothing, plucking, and whatever else.

I felt like a whole new woman by the time I opened the bathroom door to let the steam out, ready to feel the rush of cool air from the other room.

A rush that... didn't happen.

"What the hell," I muttered, stepping out into a pitch black apartment. I was energy conscious sure, but not *perfect setting for a slasher movie* vibes like this.

I grabbed one of the candles, using it to light the way for me to hurry and get some clothes on, then found my phone.

An accident on Harris Avenue has resulted in a damaged power line. Heights Municipal Services has already dispatched a crew, and will have power restored for all affected neighbors as soon as possible. Please check on young children, elders, and pets who are not able to care for themselves. There are cooling stations in place at the library and community center if you cannot safely remain in your home.

I'd gotten that message twenty minutes ago.

Right around the time my music died – which meant what I'd assumed to be a simple lost signal was actually a power outage affecting...

I hit the link in the message, pulling up the map they'd provided, marking the affected areas and the cooling stations.

Half the block was dark.

I groaned as I realized I was *already* breaking a sweat.

The weatherproofing in these old buildings was basically non-existent, so any "build up" I'd had of cool air had already dissipated.

I was going to have to open the windows.

Which, *that* shit was a task in itself.

By the time I was done, I was in a full-blown sweat, debating about the *cooling stations* for my damn self.

I did *not* feel like peopling at that level though.

Like, at all.

So, I used the last cubes the ice maker had granted to fill my water bottle and went to sit outside on the balcony, hoping to at least catch stray breeze.

What I caught was an eyeful of Calvin.

There were emergency strip lights on the balconies, solar powered. They were meant to be unobtrusive, so it wasn't enough to read or anything, but *more* than enough to see that Calvin was outside in his boxers.

Looking like a promo for... hell, *sex*.

Gosh this man is fine.

As much as I wasn't really trying to look at him *like that*, I kept running into circumstances that made it hard not to.

"You want some?" he asked, when he realized I'd stepped out.

"Some *what*?!" I replied, eyes wide until he held up what appeared to be a damn juice box.

"Oh! Uh... yeah, actually – you have another one?"

"Yuuup. You want... pineapple lemonade or fruit punch?"

"Pineapple lemonade," I answered. "Sounds like it might put me in the mind of a lemon drop." A moment later he signaled that he was tossing it to me across the short distance.

I almost dropped it, but quickly recovered.

"Good save!" he called. "I'm guessing lemon drops are your fave?"

As soon as it was in my hands, I realized it was *not* a juice box at all.

It was a frozen margarita.

"*Nice,*" I muttered, pulling off the straw and punching it into the top of the pouch. "Lemon drops *are* my fave. Thanks, neighbor!" I called to Calvin as I took a seat and kicked my feet up before I took a sip. "Although I must say – you don't give *keep girly drinks on hand at home* vibes."

He chuckled. "Leftovers from that kickback I had a few weeks ago."

"The day I moved in?"

"Yuuuup. We're probably not getting power back tonight, and it's too hot to sleep, so... may as well pretend it's a vacation, right?"

"I think I see your logic," I agreed. "But...should I be concerned that you were maybe about to sit a drink a bunch of these by yourself?"

"Nah, I just pulled out these two. My mom and sisters will probably fuck 'em up next time they slide through."

"Aww – they visit often?"

"Not nearly enough," he admitted. "I haven't had a good head rub, been told exactly where I fucked up my life, had the best thing stolen off my plate, or gotten my forehead thumped in *weeks.*"

"Whoa," I laughed. "Let me guess – baby of the family?"

"I am," he said. "Is this a case of game recognize game, or I sound spoiled or something?"

I shook my head. "Neither. You sound loved."

His eyebrows went up in surprise at that answer before he nodded. "I'll take that. What about you? You have siblings?"

"No – only child," I said. "Never met my father, but Mama has *always* held it down for me."

"We have that in common then – well, almost. Sperm donor has made his attempts to make himself known now that there's a possibility of something in it for him."

I frowned and took another sip. "That's shitty."

"Indeed. But… fuck them," he shrugged. "Like you said – Mama held it down."

"And still does," I giggled a bit. "I can't decide how I feel about it – On one hand, I would love for her to recognize that I'm a grown lady too, and can take care of myself. On the other though… girl, what time is that doctor's appointment and how am I supposed to keep this house clean *and* cook dinner? Oh, and keep myself up, and keep a roster of niggas? Cause you – she – made it look so easy."

"Oh, you've got a roster, huh?"

I sucked my teeth. "Why am I not surprised that's the only thing you heard?"

"It's not the only thing I heard – it's what piqued my interest the most," he corrected, coming to lean on the balcony railing. "Answer the question."

"If I had a *roster* of niggas, do you really think I'd be all twisted up, crying over *one*?" I asked, wrinkling my nose at him. "Besides – the point of that statement was that I do not have my shit together like she did at my age. And she had a kid!"

He chuckled. "I fully believe our parents' generation is just… I don't know. Tougher, for sure."

"Ugh, you sound like her," I groaned. "When I told

73

her what happened – after the fact, mind you, or she would've been on a plane immediately – she was *so* concerned about me being by myself in a building like this."

Calvin's head drew back. "What's wrong with this building?"

"Nothing, not really. It's just… older. She believes I *need* modern amenities or someone to help me manage *not* having them – which is why it was fine when I was living with Hunter."

Calvin laughed.

Like… a full-blown fucking *guffaw*.

"What was that for?!" I asked, mouth hanging open.

"My bad," he said, clutching a hand to his chest. "I just… having met that nigga I cannot imagine him being useful for anything uh…"

"Maintenance-y?" I filled in, and Calvin snapped his fingers.

"Yeah. That."

"Yeah – absolutely not," I laughed. "She didn't know – or hell, she probably did and was just letting me figure it out. Either *I* fixed it with help from a video I found, or it was put in a maintenance request. Which… shit, maybe that should've been a little more of a red flag than it was."

"Nah – not everybody is handy, you know? I'm not knocking him for that."

"Oh, me either," I explained. "The thing is, I *hated* that shit. Like, I would be stressed out, crying, spending my whole day on a task that would've been a twenty minute thing for a professional. And Hunter would just be off doing his own thing while I suffered."

"So why didn't y'all just put *everything* on the mainte-nance list?"

74

"Because it made him feel like a bitch," I said, rolling my eyes.

Calvin frowned. "And… having his lady stressed out over the faucet leaking *didn't*?"

"So you see the problem then," I sighed. "Anyway though… I don't want to talk about him."

"Me either," he scoffed. "Go back to what's wrong with the building."

"I already said it was nothing," I laughed. "Just normal *old building* stuff."

"Weren't you supposed to be moving into a historic brownstone though?"

"Yeah – a renovated one. With a solar backup generator."

Calvin whistled. "*Nice.*"

"Very," I agreed. "No worries about a blackout – which, my mother anticipated, by the way."

"What do you mean?"

"Well, she sends me stuff all the time – random things from her online shopping hobby. Literally a few days ago, I come home to a package. It's a damn portable air conditioner that runs on batteries and ice. Who even thinks of something like that?"

He leaned over the rail a bit, getting closer. "Wait a minute – we're out here sweating and you've got an air conditioner that doesn't need electricity?"

"Calvin… do I seem like I have what that thing needs to run?"

"Amelia… do I?"

I raised an eyebrow. "Yes, actually." We stared at each for a moment before I stood. "Bring me another one of those margaritas when you come."

"Bet."

75

9 /
amelia

NOT EVEN TEN MINUTES LATER, we were seated next to each other on my living room floor, sipping drink pouches by candlelight while that little air conditioner blew on us.

"Ay – I love your mom," Calvin said, eyes closed as he stretched his long legs out in front of him.

I giggled. "You don't even know her!"

"I know she's out here saving lives," he quipped.

"Fair enough. Thank you for setting it up – and for this second drink. These have a little kick to them. Or maybe I'm just a lightweight."

"Nah, these are definitely a two maximum situation," Calvin chuckled. "That third one would sneak up on you, so we're gonna leave it where it is."

"Probably wise."

For a moment – a long one – neither of us said anything, just enjoying our drinks and the frigid air.

"You said you were crying over that nigga?"

My eyebrows went up at Calvin's words, seemingly out of nowhere.

"Huh?"

"Earlier, out on the balcony," he said, pulling my

attention to his face in the flickering light from the candles. "When I asked if you had a roster."

"Yeah?"

"You said something like… you wouldn't be crying over the one if you had a roster."

"Something like that."

"So I'm asking… you still crying over him?"

I frowned. "I mean—"

"Hey – no judgement," he explained, holding up a hand. "I'm literally just asking."

I nodded. "Yeah, I get it. And… I guess typically… not really *over him*. More about just… the failure of it all, I guess."

"That's kinda what you were talking about this morning, right? Processing it."

"Yeah," I agreed. "And ironically… he actually hurt my feelings today."

"*Today?*"

"Mmmhmmm."

Calvin listened while I explained how I'd –kinda—run into Hunter at the coffeehouse earlier.

"So I guess it's not really that *he* hurt my feelings. More like… the situation did. Like… logically speaking, I didn't need or even *want* any acknowledgement from him necessarily, you know? But emotionally… I don't know. It's weird to spend three years of your life loving somebody, growing with them, thinking you're building a future, just to wind up… strangers in the same room."

He nodded. "Yeah… it's fucked up. This is why you didn't want to talk about him earlier?"

"Yes – and I see you couldn't help bringing him up again," I teased.

"My bad – I'm just working through my process of figuring you out. We don't have to talk about this."

I shrugged. "It's fine. The margarita has kicked in now."

"So I can ask why y'all broke up then?"

"Damn," I laughed. "Uh... Yeah, I guess. Basically, he made it known that he was unsure about the relationship – unsure about *us*. And it just... it gave me this immediate, unshakeable... *ick*. Like, if we're three years into this, I've moved in with you – at *your* request – and you're talking about you're *not sure*... we can hang this up right now before you waste any more of my time."

Calvin nodded. "So you wanted to get married, have kids, all that?"

"You know... it's not even so much that I wanted to, more that... I thought that's what we were doing. I mean, I'm not somebody that like *dreams* of that stuff, you know? Like if it happens, I would welcome that with open arms, but if it doesn't, I'll *still* have a great life."

"Then why was it such a big deal that he wasn't sure?"

"Because he'd been *acting* sure," I explained. "If you don't know how to get somewhere, we can still head in that direction, switch things up if we need to. But don't have me trusting you to get us somewhere, then we get halfway before you tell me you don't actually know – and you don't even wanna go anymore."

Calvin sighed. "I mean... I get that, but... I kinda get him too, I think. I don't believe you have to stay on a path you don't want to travel anymore just because you started walking that way."

I nodded. "I agree, actually. And I understand that people change their minds, *really*. But maybe don't let someone else uproot *their* life, change their plans, make room for you... and *then* drop the, *actually, I don't know about this* bomb. That shit was selfish."

"I can't argue with that," he admitted. "What did you say when he told you?"

"*Oh.* And then I packed my shit."

"Just like that?"

"*Just* like that," I confirmed. "My mother *always* taught me to only let a man make me feel like he didn't want me *once. You make him tell you twice, you gone understand why them folks on Snapped did what they did,*" I laughed, mimicking her voice. "And I do *not* want to go to prison behind a man."

"Solid decision-making," he said. "She taught you well."

"I like to think so too." I took the last sip from my margarita pouch and then stared at it, disappointed. "You said you had more of these?"

"Absolutely *not*," Calvin chuckled. "I already told you – no *good* decisions would come after a third one of these."

"I'd like to be the judge of that myself," I said, then immediately shivered.

"You good?" Calvin asked, eyes narrowing in concern.

I nodded. "Yeah, just starting to get a little cold, actually."

"Oh – let me help with that," he offered, moving to adjust the air con—no, actually. I *assumed* he was moving to shift the output of the air conditioner. He actually just moved closer to me, wrapping an arm around my shoulder.

Damn he smells good.

Which was a *crazy* thought to have, considering I was

basically tucked into his armpit, and we'd both been sweating. His skin was warm and dry now though, and comfortable – so much so that I reflexively relaxed into him, even as I said, "We know there were several options other than this, right?"

"Yeah, and I don't see you exploring them."

"Because you rushed at the chance to be all up on me," I countered.

"That's crazy framing when I was just trying to be a gentleman."

I sucked my teeth. "Boy please – you just wanted to touch me," I teased, tipping my head back to look into his handsome face. "Admit it."

Instead of answering, he smirked. "I don't see you rushing to get away."

"Because I was cold, duh," I said. "And you're... not."

"Well yeah, cause it's hot – and we've been drinking. I've never met anybody that gets drunk and gets cold."

I fake-gasped. "I'm not drunk," I denied, even though... I *was* feeling ever-so-slightly... *relaxed.* "This is nice."

"You sure you're not still cold?"

"Yeah... why?"

His gaze dropped, quite pointedly, to my chest. The tank top I was wearing wasn't what I would've called skimpy, especially since it had a built in bra.

That was currently not doing a damn thing about my hard nipples poking through.

Oh.

I moved my hand, intending to plant it on the floor to use as leverage to push away from him.

Instead, it landed on his thigh, and the slick fabric of

his basketball shorts moved immediately, taking my hand with it.

To his lap.

To… Is that his *dick*, I questioned myself, as my fingers – *reflexively!!* — curved around the bulge I felt.

"Damn – that's what the drinks got you on?" Calvin quipped as I snatched my hand back, and *did* then move away.

"*No*," I denied, crossing my arms over my chest to cover my nipples.

"Could've fooled me – is this why you got me over here? To take advantage of me?"

I gasped – forreal this time. "It was an accident!"

"You *accidentally* groped my dick?!"

"I… I mean… Well—"

"Relax, Sweetheart," he chuckled, shaking his head as he leaned back on his elbows. "You can touch me all you want."

I wanted to react to that, but quickly got distracted by that bulge again – something about the prominence of it…

"You're not wearing boxers, are you?"

He looked at his dick.

Looked at me.

Grinned.

And then somebody knocked on my door.

Saved by the proverbial bell.

I was quick to jump up, grateful for the distraction from an exchange that was quickly shifting into awkward territory for me. I didn't even bother checking the peephole, I just swung it open.

To find Hunter on my threshold.

"Oh!" I exclaimed. "Uh… hey?"

"Hey yourself," he said, hands tucked deep in the pockets of his sweats. He was dressed like he'd been lounging too, rounding out with slides and a tank. "I had texted, but I didn't get a response, which I mean... is cool and all, but then I thought you had maybe blocked me, so it wouldn't have gone through on your end anyway, so... here I am," he said, with a forced chuckle.

I gave him a slow nod. "Yes... here you are..."

"If you *did* block me, that's cool too... I mean... what I mean is that I get it. Of course you know it's cool, it's *your* phone—"

"Hunter... I haven't blocked you, I just wasn't on my phone. What are you doing here?"

"Right," he groaned. "My bad. I just wanted to check on you, you know... with the power being out, it's hot as fuck. Were you able to get your windows open?"

"A couple of them needed a little help – I'll make my way to the hardware store so I'm ready for next time. But, yes. I got my windows open."

"Good," he nodded. "I remember you working with the ones at our—at my place."

"Right. Is your new girlfriend in the affected area?"

Why the fuck did you ask him that, girl?!

Hunter's eyebrows went up. "Uh... nah. I'm actually about to head over to kick it at her place. Was just... making sure you were okay."

"Yeah. Well... thanks for checking on me, I guess."

"I've always tried to make sure you were good. But... I *do* get to move on, right?"

"Nigga – I didn't come to your door, you came to mine, the fuck?!" I snapped, and he immediately put up his hands.

83

"I'm talking about earlier, at UG – that look you gave me!"

I sucked my teeth. "I didn't give you a look – I dropped a dish and I was embarrassed – it was on my face when *you* looked at *me*."

He gave me that fake, close-mouthed smile people give you when they think you're a liar, and nodded.

"If you say that's what it was... okay. That's what it was."

I will put this door through your head.

"Everything good out here?"

Suddenly, Calvin's hand was at the small of my back, grazing my ass. I watched Hunter's gaze climb up, and could imagine what this looked like through his eyes.

Me standing at the door in lounge shorts and a cropped spaghetti-strap tank, nipples hard, sweat building now that I was away from the AC. Calvin behind me, tall and fine and shirtless and that tattooed copper skin contrasting against my smooth, darker tone.

I literally *watched* the vein pop up on his head.

This is lovely, really.

"Yeah," Hunter scoffed. "Everything is good."

"Cool," Calvin said, giving me a quick tap on the ass before he walked off.

I... man, okay.

"Seriously, Amelia?" Hunter chuckled – in a dry, aint-shit-funny kinda way. "So you really are fucking him? I should've known."

My eyes narrowed. "You have the nerve to comment on that wearing a hoe-fit on your way to spend the night with somebody?"

"A hoe fit?"

"That's what I said!" I hissed. "But you know – it's

none of my business, just like *he* is none of yours. Do not call, do not text, do not drop by. We don't need to do... whatever this is."

"Well excuse the fuck outta me for still giving a damn about you."

"You're excused!" I quipped, then stepped back to fling the door shut.

Wait a minute.

"I should've known."

What the *fuck* was that supposed to mean?!

My hand went to the door to snatch it back open, ready to ask some pertinent questions. But then something shifted behind me, and I turned to see Calvin standing there.

Fine ass, big dick Calvin.

"You good?" he asked.

I nodded.

"Never better."

I had the distance between us closed in two seconds flat – no thoughts, just... *impulse.*

So much impulse, lately.

But whatever.

Fuck it.

I planted hands on his shoulders and he immediately caught the vibe, sweeping me up to hook legs around his waist. I grabbed his face and took aim – my mouth on his, and not for a little peck.

His hands were on my ass, keeping me balanced as he walked me backward before my brain had even fully registered what I was doing. In the kitchen, he hiked me up on the counter, stepping between my legs to take over the kiss. I groaned as his mouth dropped to my throat, licking, sucking, *nibbling,* making my toes curl before he made his way back up.

"We need protection," I muttered against his lips, and he nodded.

Went into his pocket without breaking the kiss.

I broke the kiss, hands on his chest to push him back so I could look him in the face.

"You brought condoms with you?"

He squinted. "Uh... yes?"

"So you were *planning* to fuck me?"

"I... I mean... like just in case, you know? Trying to be responsible and prepared," he stammered.

"Oh, okay – did you bring your cell phone?"

"... no."

"Your wallet?"

"... no."

"That's not very responsible or prepared of you."

Calvin sucked his teeth. "Amelia... do you want to fuss, or do you want to fuck?"

"Both, actually," I told him, grabbing his waistband to pull him back between my legs.

He grinned over that answer, and then promptly occupied my mouth with his tongue so I *couldn't* fuss. A slow, deep kiss, with his hand between my legs, his thumb tracing my clit through my shorts.

With the low hum of that little air-conditioner trying it's best, and the flickering candlelight, it felt quite... *intimate.*

Not at all like I barely knew this man.

Not at all like this was the first time in years I'd been touched by someone who wasn't Hunter.

Not at all like I was just being reactionary, yet again.

It just felt... *good.*

Amazing, actually, to have Calvin's hand pushing those little shorts aside to sink fingers into me while his tongue was in my mouth.

That little sound he made, that satisfied grunt over how wet I was, how warm?

That was pretty damn good too, but *nothing* compared to his *"goddamn"* in my ear once that condom was on, our clothes were off, and he was finally buried inside me.

That *really* did something for me, something *really fucking good*, and so did every deep, firm stroke that followed.

Because of his height, I was barely on the counter – more like it was a backup surface in case my arms got tired of hanging on for dear life while he stroked.

Tongue on my neck.

Fingers on my clit.

Every stroke of every thing, as a whole and individually... blissful.

Truly.

At some point, I started begging – for what, I didn't even know, there was just sound pouring out of my mouth until he brought his lips to mine, kissing me between reassurances of, "I know, sweetheart. I know."

He... knew?

What the fuck did he know?

That I needed this?

That this might be the best I'd ever been fucked?

That I was *right* on the verge of coming unglued beneath him?

How did he know?

My nails dug a little harder into his skin with every roll of his hips, thighs gripped tighter on every push, trying to pull him deeper.

87

He chuckled against my lips. "I'm trying not to hurt you," he grunted.

"I think you're being stingy," I challenged.

He stopped moving.

Smirked.

Unhooked my legs from his waist to prop on his shoulders instead.

And then touched my back... from inside of me.

At least, that's what it felt like at first, so painfully deep for that half-second that I wanted to push him off me.

"*Breathe,*" he demanded, with his hands caressing my thighs as he pulled back. "I've got you."

With my fingers latched onto his arms, I did as I was told.

I breathed.

I relaxed.

When he sank into me again, it was just as deep, but my body was more accepting, honing into the contact from every nerve ending. The pull backward felt like a loss, making me clench around him to urge him not to go too far away. The re-entry was... *shit...* tear-inducing in pleasure, his dick coaxing me right back to the threshold of that coveted sweet spot.

And then shoving me through the door, growling praises about my pussy right in my ear while he fell through it with me.

For a moment, we just stayed stuck like that, heavy-breathing in each other's ear.

After a moment he let my legs down, but didn't pull out.

The AC was still humming.

Candles still flickering.

Microwave beeping, trying to alert someone to set the time.

Oh.

Oh!

"Don't act shamed now," Calvin chuckled, finally stepping back.

There were little signs all around us – including the central air kicking on – that the power had been restored, but luckily the lights out here had been turned off, helping avoid *that* particular awkwardness.

Not the rest, though.

I was suddenly hyper-aware of exactly how naked – completely – sweaty – very – and indecent – utterly -- we were. Him with the used condom, me with my legs wide open, sitting in a puddle of my own arousal.

I at least closed my legs.

Hopped down.

Looked around for the disinfectant wipes as a quick solution for now.

"Ay – you're giving off strong regret vibes, so… I'ma get outta here before you start cussing," Calvin said, as he pulled that condom off *in my damn kitchen.*

My eye twitched as I nodded. "Yeah… probably a good idea."

I was too busy finding my discarded clothes to watch him deliver that condom to the bathroom and locate his shorts.

Did I hate how I was acting right now?

Yes?

Could I help it?

Painfully, no.

I wanted nothing more than to allow myself to bask in

the fact that I'd just had my insides *so* pleasantly rearranged, and yet...

Did you really just fuck him because you were mad at Hunter? Girl... was just too prevalent on my mind, now that his dick wasn't in me.

When he stopped at the door to say something to me, I just held up a hand and shook my head.

He smirked, but left it alone.

Left.

I let out the heaviest of heavy sighs as I leaned into the door once I'd locked it behind him.

Aaaand once again, we were right back to *fuck my life.*

10 /
calvin

SHE WAS IN WITNESS PROTECTION.

Had to be.

It was the only thing that might explain how Amelia had successfully avoided me in the building for damn near a whole week since the night the power went out.

Except I'd *definitely* heard her moving around over there, so I knew she hadn't been whisked away in the middle of the night to go be a cashier in the boonies in Indiana or something.

If I could figure out a good, ignore-proof reason, I'd simply knock on the door, but I knew that would only work once fooling around with Amelia. It was basically a last-ditch effort, so I'd have to *really* make it count.

On the surface, it might look like I cared about this way too much – obviously she didn't want to be bothered, so I should respect that.

And I *could* respect it.

Would respect it.

As soon as I knew what I'd done wrong.

If she wouldn't give me anything, cool – I'd at least tried.

But I *had* to try.

My musings were interrupted by a knock at the door – a demanding-ass knock, at that. So my face was already screwed up on the way to the peep hole, and was screwed *even further* when I opened it for Arthur.

I couldn't even get the *what the hell you beating on my door like that for* out before he was already walking off, calling, "You ain't doing shit – come help me with this," over his shoulder.

"How you know if I'm doing something or not?" I asked, still frowning.

"You doin' something?"

"No."

"That's how I know – you just told me," he cackled. "Brang your ass on now, I don't have time for much conversation, got shit to do."

"This is *not* how you ask for a favor," I said, but he'd already walked through the stairwell door. Shaking my head, I pulled on the shoes I'd left by the door, stuck my phone and keys in my pocket, and followed him down.

To hell, probably, knowing him.

A few minutes later, I realized it was actually just the bottom of the stairwell, where the bolts holding the railing down had rusted and broken.

"Hold that still while I try to get this bolt outta here," he demanded, snatching off his *"Arthur's Tub & Tile"* hat to toss aside. "Damn thing shaking all over the place."

I came down the rest of the stairs, standing near to hold the railing like he needed. "There was no easier or better way than this?"

"Not when it's this far gone."

"So why let it get this far gone? Wouldn't it have been

better to take preventative measures instead of being reactionary?"

Arthur stopped struggling with the bolt to glare at me. "Who has the maintenance badge on their chest, me or you?"

"A nigga that ain't been *maintaining* shit," I countered, chuckling. "Clearly."

"You young motherfuckers are so damn disrespectful," he huffed, turning his attention back to the bolt – I realized now that the head had snapped off, and he was struggling to get it unthreaded. I offered to try it myself, and got lectured about the supposed blasphemy of a man touching another's tools.

How my inexperienced arms were just too weak for this job.

How you had to not be a dummy to not to strip the threads, and he wasn't sure I wasn't a dummy.

I... knew I should've stayed in my damn apartment.

I stood there for ten more minutes, listening to Arthur cuss and fuss at me, the bolt, the building itself, the government, the weather, and whatever else he could think to rant about.

And then he finally got that damn bolt out.

Held the two rusty-ass pieces up like they were a prize. "You see that? Sixty-two years of experience, that's what that is?"

"Sixty-two *can't* be right, for one. And for two, are you *really* going to just gloss over—"

"Here," Arthur interrupted, shoving the broken bolt in my direction, with an equally rusty washer added to the mix. "Run up there to Cooper's and grab me a replacement. Make sure it's the same size. Don't bring me no three inch bolt, you hear?"

I scoffed. "Why can't *you* go get what you need?"

"I've gotta stay here and make sure nobody gets hurt."

"You don't think a *sign* would suffice?"

"If I thought that, I wouldn't be asking you to do it."

I pulled back, chuckling. "Didn't seem like you were *asking* to me. But... whatever. I could use the fresh air anyway," I agreed, slipping the bolt pieces and washer into my pocket. "Any other requests?"

"Just to hurry it up – I got shit to do!"

"Like what? Ignoring maintenance requests until the worst-case scenario?" I quipped, they headed out the door, leaving him behind to cuss.

It would be so easy to just *not* fuck with Arthur, but honestly... there was a good chance this would be the most entertaining part of my day.

So usually, I just rolled with it.

Why not?

The walk over to *Cooper's* – which was actually *Heights Hardware & Lumber* – was only a few blocks, so it was a good opportunity to stretch my legs without being too much. Especially on a day like today – a bit of cloud cover but still sunny, a little breeze in the trees.

As such, everybody was outside.

Or at least, felt like it.

It wasn't that people in the neighborhood didn't know who I was – again, I wasn't a superstar like some of my Brawler teammates, but for a fan, I was recognizable.

Most people just left me alone.

This *wasn't* the court – I was in my neighborhood, at home, I didn't want to be mobbed, inundated with questions, none of that. It was nothing to return a wave, grin at a double-take and nod, dap up a group of teenagers on the sidewalk.

I crossed the street to avoid passing too close to the greenspace on this end – there were basketball courts, and I was *not* trying to get sucked in.

It didn't take long at all to make it to Cooper's, and once I did, I headed straight for the fastener aisle. I'd only been there a moment, hunting down the section I needed, when I heard heavy footsteps coming toward me.

I was already turning in that direction when the source of the footsteps yelled, "*Crossover!*" and hit me with my own "signature" on-court move – a quick fake to one side, then cutting back to the other before the other person even realized what was happening.

Not some shit anybody would be alert for or expecting in the middle of a damn store.

So… he got me with it.

Bad.

"In *boots* nigga?!" I huffed as I caught myself to keep from falling over my own feet. "You trying to kill me?!"

"Oh shit, my bad," Marquis cackled, holding out a fist for me to bump with mine. "I announced it and everything though, you losing your handles or something?"

My face went blank. "Why would I need *handles* among the general public?"

"Oh, that's how it is? I'm *general public*?"

"Yes, the fuck?" I laughed, finally returning his dap, and adding a quick side hug. "When did you get back in town?"

"Just a couple days ago – we've got it looking a lot better down there now."

The *down there* he was referring to was the Gulf, where recent storms had wielded a devastating level of damage

95

that impacted several majority Black communities, including some family I had down there. It was a helpless feeling, watching people that looked like you hurting, and not knowing what to do beyond sending funds. Like, that helped, sure, but it felt… distant.

When Key – Marquis – sent out the signal, saying he was gathering a group to go down and help with cleaning up and rebuilding, I was quick to answer that call.

For some selfish reasons alongside the noble ones – the timing happened to coordinate well with the end of the professional basketball season I'd been excluded from, so the tough, sometimes dangerous physical work was a great distraction.

And I got to help some people along the way, too.

There did come a point though, where my presence was noticed – in the celebrity kind of way. As "regular" as it was for me to walk around in the Heights and Blackwood, that wasn't the case down there. Media picked it up, and I had a conversation with the director of the organization we were working with and Marquis, who both agreed – it was time for me to get out of there before the headline became *Troubled Tech-foul Magnet Takes on Rebuilding Town* or some similarly dumb shit.

So I went home, earlier than planned.

Two weeks after that, Amelia moved in next door.

So… shit, maybe that was just in the grand plan.

"Good," I nodded, responding to the progress update. "I still hate that I couldn't stay longer."

Key shook his head. "You did what you could, and that's what matters man. What are you in here for though? We inspired you to take on a project with the building?"

"Nah," I scoffed. "Arthur sent me over here," I

explained, pulling the broken bolt and washer from my pocket. "Need a replacement for this."

"Let me guess – this bolt is supposed to be holding the building together, and Arthur is holding it until you get back?"

"Something like that," I laughed, turning with him to gaze at the wall of fasteners. Luckily they came in a set – bolt plus washer – so there was only one drawer to find. Key found it first, which came as no surprise.

His grandfather was the original "Cooper" the store was originally named after.

Heights Hardware was some shit Key had decided, and got talked about for.

Bad.

"Ay… somebody call you about training camp yet, or…?"

I groaned a little over that question, closing my eyes for a moment as I considered my answer – an answer I was saved from when Key spoke again.

A soft, appreciative, *"Goddamn."*

My eyes popped open, and my gaze was drawn like a beacon to the reason.

Amelia.

In her signature workout shorts and oversize tee combo, natural hair braided back into a puff, fresh face, skin glistening.

Goddamn indeed.

Her eyes went wide when she realized I was standing there, and she immediately pivoted in one direction, then another, clearly mapping her escape before she took off.

"Yo – is she… *running* from us?"

I chuckled. "Us? No. Me? Probably."

97

"Ohhhh... I don't think I've seen her before, that's you?"

"In the sense that she's off limits to *you*... yes," I answered, then started walking off, determined now to find her.

After weeks of avoidance, I didn't believe for a second that it was just "by chance" that we'd run into each other at a damn hardware store.

At the main aisle, I stopped and thought about it for a moment, searching my brain for facts that might lead me to where she was hiding out – assuming she hadn't left the store.

More likely than not, it was something for her apartment, but with it being an older building, there were myriad possibilities for things needing to be fixed.

We *did* have a little breaker overload – electricians were coming out later today to make sure it didn't happen again – but in the meantime... we'd lost air conditioning last night.

Which meant using fans, open windows...

Did she say something to me about her windows being hard to open that night I came over?

I couldn't remember.

But... I had a hunch.

I followed said hunch to HOME MAINTENANCE – weather stripping, draft stoppers, the random size batteries, and... silicon spray.

And there she was.

"Got yourself a sticky situation, neighbor?!" I called, and she didn't look up, but her grip on the can she'd been reading tightened.

Real bad.

"I've got a can of this already – you could've

borrowed mine," I told her as I approached, and she finally gave me her attention, via the *fakest* of fake smiles.

"Calvin, Hi. Funny running into you here," she gritted through her teeth as I frowned.

"Doesn't seem like you're amused at all. You seem pretty horrified, actually."

"Do I?!" she asked, high-pitched as fuck.

"You do!!" I answered back at a similar pitch, making her drop the fake smile.

"Okay – so if you *see* that I don't want to be bothered, *why* are you doing it anyway?"

"Speaking to my neighbor is *bothering*?"

She pointed the can at me like a weapon. "Now you know damn well you came to do more than speak. This is borderline stalking, actually."

"I was here first."

"And you *followed* me over *here*," she countered. "Now what?"

"You know what – now nothing," I shrugged. "You want to be pissed at me for... whatever you've decided I did wrong, what-the-fuck-ever."

"I've never said you did something wrong!"

"Well you're sure as shit acting like it," I told her. "As if you didn't want to fuck too."

"I *didn't!*" she countered, and my eyes went wide, hand to my chest, head drawn back—"Wait," she said, shaking her head. "I don't mean that like *that*," she sighed. "I'm saying... *shit*," she huffed, moving closer so we could lower our voices. "Listen... I'm not mad at *you*, I'm mad at *me*, okay?" she explained. "Are you hot? Yes. Was I curious what your dick was like? Also yes. But was I even remotely ready to be doing what we did, fresh off a breakup? *Hell no.* And the only reason I did was because

Hunter had pissed me off. Which *really* pisses me off. But again – *not* at you. At myself, for being so freaking reactionary, and I just… *oh my Goood!*" she… shrieked?

Growled?

Whimpered?

Kinda all three, but it wasn't loud, it was just… pitiful.

"It's all too much going on right now, okay?" she said, voice cracking, eyes glossy… *damn.*

"Okay," I nodded, reaching out to pull her into a – friendly – side hug. "I get it, okay? What can I do? You want to fuck again?"

"*No,*" she hissed, scooting away from me. "Did you not hear what I just said?"

I shrugged. "It wouldn't have anything to do with that cube-head ass ex. Besides – we've already done it once now anyway, so it's not like an additional body if you're trying to avoid a hoe phase or anything like that," I rationalized.

"It would be because of him, if that's the logic, because the *first* time was because of him."

"So you're saying what… I'm like… disqualified from your pussy now or something?"

"Kinda."

I sucked my teeth. "Man – that's some bullshit!"

"Seriously, Calvin?"

"It's *not* fair!"

I crossed my arms, turning away from her, just to peek back over my shoulder a moment later to catch the horrified look on her face.

And I couldn't hold my laughter.

"My goodness," she huffed, clearly relieved. "You are a fucking fool, you know that?"

"Been told a time or two," I nodded. "But to be real

clear – I *don't* think that shit is fair... just saying... but... if that's how you feel, nothing I can do but respect it. You ain't gotta dodge me though."

She blew out a sigh. "Fair enough."

I extended my arms in her direction for another hug – thinking she would blow it off, but she didn't.

She stepped right in, smelling like shea butter and oranges, and *still* I behaved myself, not pulling her closer, tighter, like I wanted to.

"*Awww*," I heard – and Amelia did too, cause she pulled back, looking around with a frown.

"*Oh, shit.*" Came next, and then *I* started looking around.

Locked eyes with Key spying on us from the next aisle.

"Really nigga?" I asked.

"Don't mind me, I just love Black love," he grinned.

"Black l—you see? This is exactly... let me get my ass out of here," she grumbled, walking off.

I looked back at Key, who tossed his hands up.

"My bad!"

11 /
amelia

TODAY IS GONNA BE *a gorgeous day.*

That was the random, delulu-as-the-solulu affirmation that popped up on my cell phone when the alarm went off to get me up.

I rolled my eyes at it before I swiped it away – not trying to be negative, but the last month had been such a whirlwhind of *not-that-gorgeous* that despite my usual purposely-sunny outlook...

I wasn't trying to hear that shit.

The day was going to be what it was going to be, and I was going to roll with it.

That was the kind of declaration that had been getting me through these days.

So... I peeled myself out of bed to see what kind of day it was gonna be.

A... great twist-out one, I soon realized once I made it to that stage of getting ready. And a phenomenal mascara one after that. I tempered myself though, refusing to get too excited.

Something could – and likely *would* go wrong at any moment.

Not the weather though – it was *such* a pretty day, with just enough cloud cover to keep it from being too hot, but still sunny and bright. A group of teenagers with designer tote bags and better lash extensions than mine told me I was "tea" as I passed them on their way to school, giving me the finger taps and all.

It... was getting harder to keep myself neutral.

I *wanted* to be optimistic, really bad.

But that's how they trick you.

Who the fuck was "they"?

Who knew?

But, by the time I sat down at Urban Grind after securing the last butter roll from the bakery case – a truly baffling stroke of luck – I was *sure*.

They were definitely on my ass.

I had to keep my eyes open.

A notification popped up on my screen, and as soon as I realized what it was – an email from Proxy's Media Relations Manager – my shoulders sank.

I knew it.

I took a deep breath before I opened the message, steeling myself for whatever the correspondence held.

A... glowing, unexpected shout-out in *Sugar&Spice* magazine.

That was what it held.

I really need to seek help.

As hard as I tried, all day, to find some gloom that might support my reticence to just *chill*... I simply could not.

It was great.

The KANAOS class was great, and I got a massage after, got my nails and brows done. By the time I was heading back to my apartment for the day, the sun was setting, painting the sky over the Heights a beautiful mixture of red and purple and orange and pink. Somebody had a grill going, and the smell drove me to the corner store at the end of my block.

I got the last plate of burnt ends, and they gave me the extra that wasn't enough to make another.

That was the last straw.

I was over the moon by the time I made it back to my building – in such a good mood that when I saw Calvin outside on that cracked court, running his usual solo drills, I didn't avoid him.

I went and sat down on the steps.

And just... watched him.

He was *always* working out, like he was training for something. Even since the hardware store, nearly a week ago, it seemed like he was ramping up his conditioning.

I wasn't into sports, not even in the slightest, and still I could tell – he was made for this. He was fast, fluid, but always in total control. His shots slid through the creaky hoop like butter, he seemed to always know exactly where the ball was going to go.

All this while shirtless.

Nice.

"Enjoying the show?"

My eyes went wide when I realized he was talking to me – apparently he'd stopped moving, had the ball tucked under his arm, and was standing right in front of me.

Grinning.

Oops.

Guess I'd locked in a little too hard on that one particular titty-sweat trail dripping down his rib tats.

"Yes, actually," I answered with a shrug.

That grin of his stretched even wider, and he leaned in, probably about to say something that was going to make my face hot.

But... his phone rang.

A very corporate-sounding tone I wouldn't have expected from him.

One that made the humor immediately dropped from his face as he pawed at the zippered pocket on his shorts to retrieve the device.

A glance at the screen shifted his expression again – panic, relief, uncertainty all at once – and he gestured for me to hold on while he hit the button to answer and raised the phone to his ear.

"Tell me something good, Boss Lady," he greeted – there was nothing flirtatious about the tone, but still... interesting way to open a phone call. I couldn't hear the other end, but then Calvin spoke again. "What about the contract?"

Ooop.

This is not my business at all.

I was up on my feet in record time, giving Calvin a wave to acknowledge that I was going upstairs instead of hanging around.

I didn't want to be nosy.

So as soon as I was settled at my counter with my plate, I googled my neighbor.

I'd called the man things that weren't his given name over this time.

Noise Violation.

Big Dick Calvin.

This Motherfucker.

And apparently, the internet had another name for him.

Crossover.

Calvin "Crossover" Cross.

Headlines.

Stats.

Highlight reels.

Pictures giving out turkeys.

And... a bit of scandal.

A bit of *"promising career cut short"* talk that I was waffling on investigating further.

Today's vibes had been *so* immaculate... was I really about to take a hard left?

No.

No, I wasn't.

I called Kaelyn instead.

She answered on the second ring, bonnet and pimple patches on for the night, ice cream spoon in hand. "Bestii-iieee," she sang, then squinted at the screen. "Wait – why do you look like that?"

I frowned, looking down at my clothes and then back up. "Like what?"

"Like you just found out Big Mama sold the house."

I sucked my teeth. "Shut up," I laughed. "I just... found out something I feel insane for not already knowing?"

"Okay..." she sat up a bit, and I realized she was stretched out on her couch at home. "So spill the beans?"

I sighed. "So... you know how the night we had that blackout over here... I slept with my neighbor?"

"The neighbor you've been being all secretive about that nigga's name?!"

"Because you would've done everything but a background check, and I wasn't trying to get that involved!"

"I do the background check now too, first of all," Kae said, jabbing her spoon at the screen. "And second – that man has had his dick in you, I don't know how much more *involved* it gets!"

"You know what I mean."

"I know you've been self-sabotaging cause Hunter fucked your head up."

I gasped. "Self-sabotaging how!?"

"Bitch! Are you *not* in a whole... whatever you wanna call this thing with your stranger danger neighbor?!"

"He's not a stranger! And there's no *thing*."

"It's a thing, Ames. It's definitely a thing."

"It's definitely *not* a thing, excuse you. Can I say what I called to say, damn!"

"Say it then!" Kae laughed, eating another spoon of ice cream.

"Thank you!" I huffed, pausing for –infuriating, based on Kae's expression – dramatic effect before I said, "Girl why is this nigga a whole professional basketball player?"

She blinked.

Blinked again.

"I'm sorry... what? I thought I heard you say the "random" neighbor you're fucking is a professional basketball player?!"

"I did!"

"Girl, *what?!*" she shrieked. And then, "*Who?!*"

"Calvin Cross."

"The Crossover?!" she yelled, standing up from her seat. She fumbled with the phone a second before it came with her, putting her face back into view. "Amelia... you didn't know?!"

"Kae – do I *seem* like the type of bitch that would know?!"

She laughed. "I mean... generally speaking, no. He's not like... superstar level like a Kevion Ward, but girl... I know Hunter hates your ass."

"What does he have to do with it?"

The grin slid off her face. "Wait... so... if you didn't know who Calvin was... oh, friend."

"Oh my God, *what??*"

"Do you remember that time I came and stayed in the Heights with you – you had moved in with Hunter already, but he was going out with his friends."

I nodded. "Yeah, they went to a Brawler game, and like a party after or something. They stayed in Blackwood."

"Yes, that's exactly the night I'm talking about. I was there when Hunter left to go out... wearing a Brawlers jersey. More specifically, wearing a *Calvin Cross* jersey."

"Nooooo!"

"Oh *yes*," Kae started cackling. "I remember because Calvin got in major freaking trouble that same night – suspended for the rest of the season, actually. It was a big deal, and I meant to ask Hunter about it, but... I don't like talking his ass, so I just didn't."

"Oh my goodness, *no wonder* he's been so damn *pressed* about every interaction."

"Not you fucking on his favorite playerrrrr,"

"Not on purpose!" I defended, but she just kept laughing.

"That's what makes it so good. Oh man... what a great turn of events."

"Kae!"

"What?!"

"That's so mean. I'm *mortified*."

She sucked her teeth. "Whatever. Didn't you say Hunter already had a new boo anyway?"

"Yeah, but—"

"But nothing," Kae spoke up. "You didn't do anything wrong. It's not *your* fault he lost his girl *and* his favorite player – he can take it up with whoever he pissed off enough to stick them needles—"

Mid-rant, a knock sounded at the door.

A fresh grin spread over Kae's face. "Is that him?"

I didn't even know which *him* she was referring to, but I desperately hoped it was neither as I made my way to the door to peek out.

Calvin.

Still with no shirt on.

"Okay I'll talk to you later," I told Kae, who immediately burst into a fit of giggles. "Oooh, she's getting off the phone to talk to her booooo!"

"Oh my God, *shut up*," I hissed, then ended the call, hoping like hell Calvin hadn't heard her loud ass through the door.

I stowed the phone in my pocket, then unlocked and opened it to find him grinning.

"You know I heard your loud ass friend, right?"

Of course he had.

"How can I help you?" I asked, instead of entertaining *that* at all, since Calvin was a little too slick at the mouth for me to not get caught up. "Oh!" I quipped, eyes wide, as he welcomed himself inside before turning to me to raise and flex his arms.

"Guess who gets to start training camp next week?" he boasted, making me laugh.

110

"Congratulations, I'm assuming?" I replied. "That's a good thing, right?"

He frowned at me a moment before shaking his head. "Damn, you *really* don't fuck with the sportsball, huh?"

"I don't" I admitted. "But, I *love* that for you... I think?"

"Yes," he nodded. "It's a good thing. That call I got, it was from my agent, so I couldn't let it get past me. Sorry for interrupting our conversation though."

I raised an eyebrow. "Was it a conversation?"

"It was certainly *about* to be," he said, moving closer to me. "Something about you admiring my elite athletic physique... remember?"

"Not even a little." I crossed my arms. "Back to important matters – you were worried about not getting invited to training camp? That's like... summer practice?"

He scoffed. "More like fucking... tryouts. I'm being given a chance to earn back my spot on the team."

"Which is...?"

"Shooting guard," he said. "Although, technically, that's not really—"

"Please don't... I'm not gonna have any idea what you're talking about," I said, stopping him before he launched into whatever technicality he was about to explain. "What do you *do*?"

He laughed. "Uh... make buckets, and make however is trying to keep me from making said buckets look silly whenever I can."

"Okay, *that* I understand... I think. But... and forgive me if this is too nosy, but that sounds super important. So... if you were responsible for that... why do you need to prove yourself to the team?" I asked. "Like... why do you have to *earn back* your spot?"

111

Calvin sighed, shoving his hands into the pockets of his shorts. "Uh... I got suspended from the league a few months ago – couldn't finish the season."

"Damn – what did you do?!"

"Uh..." he blew out *another* sigh. "I kinda... punched a coach, mid-game."

My eyes went wide.

I *didn't* fuck with the sportsball, and even *I* knew...

"Yeah, it was pretty bad," he agreed, nodding. "I still feel like I actually didn't do enough, but I probably would've gotten banned... and arrested... so... everything considered, it went as well as it could."

"Calvin... now why the hell would you *punch* a coach?!" I asked. "The other team?!"

"Nah. One of mine," he admitted. "But in my defense... I warned his ass it was coming."

I shook my head. "My mind is blown – you punched one of your coaches and you're still on the team?"

"I'm still on *contract*," he corrected me. "On the team is yet to be determined, which is why... training camp."

"I get that part, but still. Everybody must not like him or something?"

"Literally the most punchable nigga on the planet," Calvin explained. "My *head* coach wasn't even mad like that for real, but it was *conduct unbecoming* or some bullshit. As if *his* ass wasn't... you know what, never mind, before I get pissed all over again," he chuckled, and I nodded.

"Fair enough. *But...* I'm dying to know what was the last straw?" I kinda whispered. "You can tell me to mind my business, I won't be offended."

"Nah," he shook his head. "I'm not trying to get into it too deep, but he said some slick shit about something...

deeply personal, deeply private, deeply nothing to do with him, or the team, none of that. But he decided mid game, Trojans handing us our ass in a frilly basket, everybody already stressed the fuck out, to say something that was... too fucked up for me to let slide. So I didn't."

"You know... I love a good standing on business moment myself, so I can't even blame you," I said. "And I really hope you do amazing at training camp – how was their season without you?"

He smirked. "I'm not saying it's because I wasn't there, but the three seasons before this, I *was* there, and we at *least* made the finals."

"Oh they're missing you bad."

"I may have heard a little of that from my teammates. But you know... we'll see. I'm looking forward to proving myself," he said, heading for the door unprompted. "Appreciate the pep talk, Sunshine."

I grinned. "Ohhh, I'm not *Pissy* today?"

"Nah, you're on a different energy today – good vibes."

"Don't get too used to it," I quipped as I opened the door to see him out. "I punch niggas too."

His eyes went wide, and I laughed. "That was supposed to be a joke."

"Hahhahah," he deadpanned, then grinned, and I just closed the door.

Damn.

Today *was* a really good day.

12 /
amelia

"Now, you know I don't believe that shit for a second, right?"

My mouth dropped in a fake gasp – wait, not fake, just not like...

Okay.

Fake.

It was fake.

I was nowhere near surprised Claire wasn't buying my *"it's nothing, really"* insistence where Calvin was concerned when I barely believed it myself.

As much as I could though, I was enjoying the view from my riverfront home on Denial.

I shook my head, bumping her shoulder with mine as I leaned into her in our booth at Hideaway. "It has barely been a month since the breakup with Hunter. What kind of classy woman of high moral standard would I be if I was already moving on to someone else?" I asked, picking up my lemon drop.

"Okay, first of all, since *when* were you trying to be *that?* Second... I thought you fucked him on your kitchen counter a few weeks ago?"

115

I choked on the lemon drop.

"Well, *yes*," I admitted, since she already knew all the details anyway. "But like... I'm trying to tighten up."

"For what?"

"*Life*," I laughed. "I don't know... I just... I feel like, okay... it's been a month... I've gone a week without crying about the breakup... okay, let's put things back on track."

Claire nodded. "Including this thing with you and the basketball player."

"There's no *thing*. Why are you and Kae trying so hard to make it a *thing*?"

Claire's lips pressed together, eyes narrowed before she scoffed, suppressing a laugh. "Okay Amelia. Define it however you'd like. I'm listening."

"We're friends!"

"Me and you? For sure. For *life*," Claire insisted, grabbing and squeezing my hand before I snatched it away from her.

"Me and *Calvin*, you knew what I meant!" I laughed as she covered her face, trying to hide her clear teasing.

"I'm just saying... your definition of *friends* is a lil' different than what happens in *my* head when I think of that word. I mean... you and I are friends, and I've never been knee-deep in your p—"

"*Sinclaire!*" I squealed, eyes wide. "Why are you— hold on," I muttered as my phone buzzed in my lap, and I picked it up to look at the screen.

Specifically... to read a text.

From... Calvin.

"See?" Sinclaire drawled, leaning into me to peek at the phone. "You've been showing every tooth in your mouth every time that phone goes off, all night."

I shrugged. "I can't help it, he's funny!"

"And if you keep laughing, his stand up-routine is going take residence in your panties."

I sucked my teeth. "I'll have you know, he has not made a single attempt at sex since we exchanged numbers."

To prove my point, I held up the screen, showing her the thread of messages between us from the past week.

It was quite random, actually.

... charmingly so.

Jokes about Arthur's antics, complaints about what *Fresh* was out of, roasting each other's food choices, *complimenting* design choices, music recommendations, basketball explanations...

Like friends.

Just friends.

It was refreshing.

And endearing.

"Wow," Claire mused, nodding as she looked away from the phone, back to me. "That is not at all what I expected. That looks like *our* thread. And it's way less problematic than our group chat with Kae."

"That's what I'm saying," I laughed. "You thought I was lying?"

"*Lying* sounds so harsh," she replied. "I would have said... deluding yourself?"

"*Wooow.*"

"Wait," she said, grabbing my hand. "Not like in a bad way, just... we do that sometimes – convince ourselves that what we're feeling isn't what we're feeling because we're not "supposed" to be feeling it. You know what I mean?"

I scoffed. "All too well – I was *very* delusional with Hunter, self-imposed."

Claire sighed. "How are you feeling about that now? We started talking about it and then took a left."

"I'm okay – like I said – no tears for a whole week. I don't miss him. I'm not really even angry about it – not on a day to day kind of thing at least. I'm good. *Really.*"

She raised an eyebrow at me. "For real really, or your toxic positivity, fake-it-til-you-make-it really?"

"*Real* really," I laughed. "Besides – I think I give up on toxic positivity – that shit doesn't work when your life is *actually* in shambles."

"No shit," she quipped. "Why do you think I was ready to wring your neck when you were on that kumbaya shit after ol' girl was copying my videos bar-for-bar and making more money off them than I was?"

"Uh, in my defense, you developed a stress ulcer and had the scariest panic attack I've ever seen before in my life – I thought you were going to die, friend."

"Fair enough," Claire admitted. "But can you see how that was *not* it now?"

I nodded. "Grudgingly, I do. And I'm sorry."

"No worries – we're all just muddling through the best we can," she said, then glanced at her own phone as a notification came in. "Oh, my Proxy ride is here – are you *sure* you won't just share the ride with me?"

I sucked my teeth. "It's the complete opposite direction, and besides – it's only like a ten minute walk from here."

"Yeah, at night, in Old Heights."

"*Old Heights*," I mimicked, wrinkling my nose. "Okay *snobbery.*"

"It is *not* snobbery, thank you, it is simply common

sense," Claire argued. "Babe, there's parts of Blackwood I don't go without that thang on me either."

I smirked. "Not gentrified enough for the big city girl?"

"Okay can you stop, with the *bougie* edit on me? Like I don't literally make my living building and repairing stuff on camera? I'll actually have you know, I'm looking at a rowhome... in *Old Heights*."

My eyes went wide. "Reallllly?! We're gonna be neighbors?!"

"I don't know... it's in *really* bad shape, but it would make great content," she mused.

"Worse than the building I'm in?"

"Ames!" she laughed. "You're in the Foundry – it's a perfectly fine building, just old. It's in good shape mostly. Just a little bit down Timberline though... *those*."

"The rowhomes the teenagers around here claim are haunted?!"

"Yessss," she replied. "Tell me that series wouldn't go crazy!"

"Yeah, I see it now – you in your pink hard hat and belt... getting carted off to hell by Casper. That shit will instantly go viral."

"Bye!" Claire laughed, standing from her seat. "Let me get out here before my ride leaves – also... bring your ass. We had one too many drinks for me to feel comfortable with you walking. And I'm *not* arguing with you, just come on."

I rolled my eyes about it, but stood too, taking her up on the offer to share the *Proxy* ride. When I was already stepping through the door of the building five minutes later instead of just being halfway through my walk, I was *very* glad i had.

119

Maybe even more so when I rounded the corner for the elevator just as Calvin was stepping on.

He saw me as he turned to put his back to the elevator wall, grinned, and immediately reached out to press the button.

To close the elevator.

"*Seriously?!*" I yelled as he cackled loud enough for me to hear him through the metal doors. It didn't take long at all for the elevator to come back since it was just one floor up, but it was still annoying.

Especially since I'd been lowkey happy to run into him.

Especially when his grinning face was the first thing I saw when the elevator opened on our floor.

"Boy get the fuck on somewhere," I told him, pushing past his open arms as I silently warred with myself over the smile threatening to break free.

"Wait, don't be mad," he laughed as he followed me. "What's the matter, you not in a playing mood?"

I huffed. "I was in a *great* mood, actually, until you pulled that shit."

"Daaamn, I killed the vibe? My bad," he told me as we reached our adjacent doors. "How can I make it up to you?"

"*Hmmm,*" I said with an exaggerated sigh, and a finger on my chin like I was actually thinking about it. "You could... go in your house and leave me alone?"

His grin faltered, and then his eyebrows furrowed as he fixed me with a worried gaze. "Hold up... you're *actually* mad?"

I sucked my teeth. "No," I admitted, chuckling as I fumbled with my keys. "That shit *was* annoying though."

"My bad. Where you coming from this late, looking this good?"

"Drinks with a friend," I answered, giving him a little up-and-down before I said, "same question for you."

"Dinner meeting in Blackwood with my agents."

"Agents... plural?"

"Yeah, kinda. Well – it's an agency, and they handle their athletes like a group project... kinda. I don't fully understand the business model, but it's been working for them, and working for me, so... no complaints."

I nodded. "Dinner is a good thing though, right?"

"Not getting dropped for misconduct is the good thing."

I leaned against my –now open – doorframe, crossing my arms. "*Misconduct...* the big secret you can't reveal?"

"What?" he chuckled. "I... I wouldn't call it a big secret."

"You treat it like one."

His eyebrows went up. "Do I?"

I nodded.

"Oh. Damn. I just don't really like talking about it, but I wouldn't call it a secret – I told you I punched the coach. That shit was on live TV. I got *memed.*"

"Yeah, but you never said *why*... and the internet speculated, but I mean... it's the internet."

He smirked. "And what did *the internet* say?"

"A wild array of things that felt increasingly inaccurate the more I get to know you."

"Okay... what about the one that your gut told you was might really be it?" he asked, and my eyebrows went up.

There *had* been one of those.

I sighed, wetting my lips with my tongue before I

121

answered. "It was about your dad. Something mean. Something I would've busted him in his shit for too. Something anybody would've."

Calvin chuckled. "Yeah. Probably why I'm being asked back."

"So... is it true?" I asked.

He shrugged. "I still don't know exactly what you heard, and you're obviously trying not to cross the line into nosy, so you're not outright saying it, so... I don't know. But, if the internet is saying I socked ol' boy for telling me he "would've let my ass with my momma to fend for ourselves just like my crackhead daddy did"... then yeah, it's true."

I... snapped my mouth shut.

I didn't even know it was open.

I was... *baffled*.

"You're serious?" I asked. "A *coach* said that to you? Unprompted?"

Calvin squinted. "I wouldn't say *unprompted*," he chuckled. "I might've called him a bitch or something before that, we were going back and forth. But he took it to hell and I caught a ride."

"Rightfully," I nodded.

"So... was that it? Is that what the streets are saying?"

"Not that I saw," I told him. "What I saw was about your dad maybe having the substance abuse issue, which was bad enough, really. I would never imagine someone from your team throwing such a thing in your face like that."

Calvin smirked. "There... may also have been a woman involved. Pussy brings out the worst in niggas."

"Oh is that right?" I laughed. "Who snatched whose woman?"

"I don't know about *snatched*," he answered. "But his ex-wife was one of the physical therapists on the team. He wasn't feeling the special sessions she was giving me, so he was picking with me."

"Now how did y'all keep *that* part off the internet?!" I asked, shocked.

"That was nobody but RSM," he chuckled.

"RSM?"

"Richardson Sports Management," he explained.

"Ahhh," I nodded. "Understood. So all of that, and it still ended up that you got painted as a hothead and he's moved on to another team."

He shrugged. "People love the headlines more than they love the truth... and sometimes it's best to just let it be."

"Fair enough," I said. "Well... thank you for sharing the truth with me, at least."

Calvin grinned, then reached out and... booped me on the fucking nose. "That's what friends are for, right? G'night, Li-Li."

And then before I could really react to *any* of that, he was inside his apartment.

Clearly running away from the conversation.

All I could do was go inside and close my door too.

And reflect.

Did he really just boop me on my fucking nose?

123

13 /
calvin

A WEEK.

Training camp starts in just about a week.

Fuccck.

Why did that sentence set off a nervous buzz that settled in my stomach like I was some fresh recruit?

This wasn't my first training camp.

It wasn't even my *fifth* training camp.

I wasn't at "seasoned vet" status yet, but I was no rookie either – if that bullshit with Coach Lewis hadn't happened, last season would've been the one that *did* turn me into a household name.

I'd been on fire, and all it took was a little fuel from my sperm donor to give Coach Lewis the ammo he needed to douse me out.

Over a woman who'd used me as a sentient dildo.

Not that I hadn't fully enjoyed myself, but it was crazy that ol' boy had crashed out so hard over me fucking his ex wife when it was *purely* that.

Crazy ass chain of events, period.

And now here I was, feeling the effects of my own

poor decision making with my appendages – I'd promised myself since then to be a little more careful.

Promised my *mother* I'd be a little more careful.

A loud *thump* from next door pulled my attention away from the calendar I'd been reviewing on my laptop to my shared wall with Amelia.

What the hell is she doing over there?

I shook my head.

Nope.

Whatever her fine ass had going on over there was not my business – I was *not* supposed to be seeking interaction.

We were neighbors.

Friendly neighbors.

Friends.

That's it.

All it *needed* to be, for both of our sakes to be honest.

I shifted my attention back to my screen.

Training camp in a week.

The RSM mixer in a few days.

Training camp was going to be my first time with a ball in my hand in an official capacity in months, but the mixer... that was work, too.

It wasn't an official team event, but many of my team-mates would be there, because they were signed to Richardson Sports Management as well. They always held it at this time of year, right in this little pocket where most major sports were in a quiet period, which meant they could have their big party with all their athletes, their spouses, and plenty of others adjacent to the professional sports industry.

Deals got made at this party.

Connections got made at this party.

Relationships – the romantic type -- got made at this party.

That was the part I was feeling kinda iffy about, honestly speaking. It was always teeming with fine ass single women, which wasn't the worst thing to happen to a man, but damn.

It was never on any quick-hit, groupie type shit either.

They were trying to get locked down, trying to make a ring-worthy first impression they could cash in on later. And while I respected the hustle, I simply wasn't on that type of time, so I wasn't interested in the whole, *come meet this friend* set up.

Jordan and Cole – the Richardson-Johnson's of the *R* in RSM – might not like it, but I was strongly considering simply skipping it, to avoid dealing with that shit all night.

But how would that reflect in other areas?

I was mulling that over when another, louder thump came from next door, paired with an unmistakable, feminine *"ouch!"*

I was on my feet before I could even stop myself.

Seconds later, I was knocking on Amelia's door, and getting worried when I didn't get an immediate answer. I knocked again, fully prepared to force my way in when the door finally cracked open, and Amelia peeked out.

"Yes?" she answered, clearly out of breath – eyes wide, hair uncharacteristically disheveled.

"Everything okay?" I asked, trying to peek behind her, but she moved so only a sliver of the door was open.

"Mmhm!" she squeaked – voice entirely too high – "Why do you ask?"

My eyes narrowed, and then I immediately just pushed past her, stepping in to look around.

"Excuse you!" she fussed behind me, but didn't try any harder to stop my progress into her apartment. "What the hell are you doing?"

"Seeing what the hell is going on," I answered, scowling as I turned to her. "I heard thumping, heard you get hurt—"

"Wait – did you think somebody else was in here?" she asked, crossing her arms.

I shrugged. "Just making sure."

"So you ran in my house half naked ready to kick ass cause you heard me say *ouch*? That's so..."

"Chivalrous? Admirable? Gener—"

"*Obsessed*," she laughed. "You're *so* obsessed with me!"

"I... man, whatever," I chuckled too, shaking my head. "This is how you thank me for making sure some nigga wasn't in here knocking your head into the dishwasher?"

She sucked her teeth. "You know what – you're right, Calvin. Thank you. Now if you'll excuse me... neither of us is dressed for company, so..."

Now that she'd brought up my level of undress a second time, I looked down at myself – I was, indeed, in just my boxers. She was in boy short panties and a sports bra.

So... okay, we were both in our underwear.

I guess I got her point.

And then, looking past her, I *got* what all the racket was about.

"You trying to break something?" I asked, pointing to the half-assembled basket-chair-swing thing laying on the ground, and the pastel-handled tools strewn about the floor. I saw the big ass hook… the coffee table pulled to an awkward spot… no ladder… "Amelia…"

"What?" she replied, voice all fake-innocent, eyes wide.

"Did you fall off that damn table?"

She raised her hands like she was confused. "What table?"

"*That* table!" I pointed. "Don't piss me off right now."

"Why are you being mean to me?!" she huffed, crossing her arms – this time, I caught the quick, pained expression as she did.

"Nobody is being mean to your silly ass," I replied, moving closer to look at her arm. "You wouldn't be able to fake like you aren't in here being reckless if it was broken, so at least there's that," I said as I surveyed her.

"Dramatic," she accused. "It's nothing a little ice won't fix."

"Because you got lucky. Why are you trying to put that thing up anyway – I didn't think you wanted to get quite so settled in."

She sighed. "Well, yeah, that was the plan, and then I found out that the whole *dream brownstone* thing is looking more like a nightmare – they found *mold*."

"Ugh."

"Yeah, exactly," she nodded. "So… after that bit of bad news, I figured I would do something that made me happy – and putting up this chair would really make me happy, I think. I talked to Claire, and she gave me some tips and stuff, helped me find the right beam to hang it from… I just don't have a ladder. I thought between the table and me on my tiptoes…"

"Nah," I chuckled. "You know you could've shot me a text, right?"

She wrinkled her nose. "I didn't want to overstep."

"Overstep?" I scoffed. "We text about every other random thing."

"Yeah, but... this is a little different. Hanging stuff, building furniture... that's getting into *favor* territory, and I know how niggas get."

My eyes went wide. "Enlighten me. How do we get?"

"Pervy," she answered, shrugging. "You ask a male "friend" for a favor, and it's a well known fact that you risk him wanting a *favor* in return."

I frowned. "What's wrong with that? I scratch your back, you scratch mine!"

"If it was *drive me to the airport, pick up a gallon of milk for me* it would be fine. Y'all have a tendency to want *ass* though."

"Oh, shit," I chuckled. "I... can understand your hesitation when you put it like that," I admitted. "But you know I'm not on any shit like that with you, right?"

She gave me a deadpan look. "Prove it."

"How am I supposed to prove that?"

A little flash of mischief crossed her face as she smirked, grabbing my arm with both hands. "Calvin... could you *please* help me install this chair?" she asked, fluttering her eyelashes at me and all.

Damn, I was easy.

"Yes," I agreed, grinning. "And I already know how you can return the favor."

Her eyes narrowed. "How?"

"I install this chair for you... you come to this work party with me."

"Work? As in... basketball?"

I nodded. "Yeah. You get to dress up, probably meet some celebrities... very nice gift bag," I explained.

"Only catch is that you have to pretend to be my girlfriend."

She wrinkled her nose. "How nice is the gift bag?"

"Last one had a *Moments&Measures* watch, a bottle of *Kimble Reserve*, and a gift card to *Nectar*. And that's just the stuff I kept – I gave my sister a bunch of girl shit that was in there."

Amelia nodded. "How nice of a dress up? Are we talking gala or cocktail?"

"Cocktail."

"Mmhm. Hm…," she mused. "But having to pretend to *like* you… it better be a *good* ass gift bag."

I scoffed. "Lie to yourself all you want, Li-Li. I'll go grab a ladder."

A few minutes later I was back – and clothed in some shorts and a tee shirt.

Amelia had put on another layer as well, and together we made pretty quick work of getting that hook securely mounted, and then getting the chair itself in place.

"Okay… moment of truth," I said, stepping back to admire our efforts.

"You sure it's in there?" Amelia asked, and I chuckled.

"How many times did you fall before I got over here?"

"Why are you so focused on the past?" she countered with a smirk, then moved to take a seat in the chair – gingerly at first, and then sinking in. "It *feels* secure at least."

I met her gaze. "Good. Let's test it."

Her eyes went wide, hands up, but I'd already given the chair a nice hard push, sending her swinging – and yelling about it.

"Calvin!" she shrilled, and I laughed as I caught the chair, stopping the momentum. "That wasn't funny!"

131

"You're right – it was *hilarious*," I countered, grinning still as she glared at me from her newly-installed throne.

"What if I had fallen?"

"Wouldn't have happened – this thing is in there solid as a rock. You're welcome, by the way."

She stopped glaring to roll her eyes. "Thank you, I guess."

"You guess?"

"Fine – I *know*," she amended, a soft smile spreading over her lips as she leaned back, letting the chair settle into a slight sway. "Thank you. I do feel a tiny bit better. This is… a vibe."

I studied her for a second before I nodded.

That smile of hers was… dangerous.

"Yeah… definitely a vibe."

That look lingered too long.

Instead of letting it get awkward though, I grabbed the sides of the chair again. Immediately, Amelia put a foot out, planting it against my chest to push away from me. "Stoooop!" she insisted, and I laughed.

"I'm just fucking around. I wasn't gonna do it."

"You're a menace," she laughed, as I grabbed her foot… and yanked like I was going to pull her out of the chair. "See?!" she screamed as I let her go, clutching the sides of the chair.

"Relaaaax," I chuckled. "I'm gonna leave you alone. You enjoy your chair."

"I plan on it – thank you again," she said, still smiling as I backed away.

That pretty ass smile.

Damn.

"Uh… I'll text you the details for the party?"

"Yeah, for sure," she agreed, sinking back into the chair.

At peace.

It was good to see, and I stood there for probably a bit longer than I should, thinking about how easily I would've hung a hundred fucking chairs for her, just to see her like this.

And then I got my ass out of there, to get my mind right again.

Training camp in a week.

Mixer in a few days.

... and a fine ass neighbor I could easily get way too wrapped up in *right now.*

14 /
amelia

"So we're all in agreement – this is the one, right?" I asked as I surveyed myself in the mirror once more.

"I stepped away from the screen, but the yellow midi is the only real option," Kae called out.

When I peeked at my own screen, sure enough, Claire's face was visible, but Kae wasn't.

"She's wearing the yellow one," Claire confirmed for Kae, giving me approving nod. "Calvin is going to choke on his tongue when he sees you – in a good way."

I grinned, turning back to the mirror.

This was the *sixth* dress I'd pulled from my closet, from a section of dresses I'd never worn. Apparently I'd just been collecting them, waiting for a date night with Hunter that never came because he trended toward busy or wanting to do things I had zero interest in. I'd been determined not to buy anything new, even though Calvin had offered to cover it.

He'd actually offered to pay for anything I wanted – beauty services, shoes, jewelry, dress, whatever I needed to feel good for tonight.

Too bad all my maintenance appointments had been a few days before.

And again – I had a closet full of things I'd never *gotten* to wear, so it was more fun for me to *not* spend the money.

Though... the ease with which he'd offered was endearing.

But hell... what *wasn't* endearing about Calvin at this point?

"Not you looking like a nervous teenager headed out for a first date," Kae laughed. When I looked back, she'd returned to the screen, with a facial treatment mask on now.

I sucked my teeth. "Not y'all insisting on seeing me off like proud parents."

"Oh I'm definitely proud, personally," Claire spoke up. "A chance to meet Sierra Ward on a first date, a month after a breakup? This is the way."

"It's not a date," I corrected. "I'm doing Calvin a favor, because he did me a favor."

"That doesn't make it not a date." Kae grinned. "And that dress makes it *absolutely* a date."

I smirked at myself in the mirror.

The square neckline toed the line of too much cleavage, and the fit was *right* on the border of slutty. My back was fully covered though, and the "midi" length brought it past my knees – classy. A simple, tasteful strappy heel, no jewelry to distract from my pretty ass skin, natural mane pulled into a little updo with a few curls hanging down...

Yeah.

Yeah.

I looked good.

"So how far are y'all taking the *favor*," Kae asked. "Do y'all have a story planned for how y'all met?"

"Oooh," Claire chimed in. "Cause you know people are going to be nosy."

"We decided some honesty is the best policy," I explained, moving over to my dresser for perfume. "With me coming off the breakup with Hunter, we can't lie that we've "been together" longer than we have."

"Good point – if this goes around social media, you'd get labeled and cheater," Kae agreed.

"Trollop."

"Whore."

"Jezebel."

"I get it," I laughed, stopping their back and forth. "And, yeah, exactly. So we're going to lean into it being... like a new discovery, you know?"

"Oh so you're just telling the truth," Claire quipped.

I sucked my teeth. "No, because the *truth* is that we're friends, and that's all."

"Girl you not tired of that lie yet?"

"*Lie* is crazy, wow," I laughed, stepping through a final mist of my favorite perfume. It was a small batch, indie release from Tempest at *Wax Poetic* – her spin on her *own* favorite perfume. I had it in candle form already, and used those often, but the perfume was limited, and therefore... coveted.

Special occasions only.

Like this date.

Damn.

I didn't get a chance to process my realization *or* respond to my friends' teasing – a knock sounded at the door. Immediately, I realized I couldn't hear Calvin's –

respectfully leveled -- music through the wall anymore, which meant he was done getting ready.

And at the door to pick me up.

"Girl, your *face*," Claire cackled, scaring me for a moment until Kae laughed too.

"What?!" I asked, confused as I checked myself in the mirror. "What's wrong?"

"Nothing," Kae giggled. "I've just never seen anybody light up like you just did when that nigga knocked on the door."

"Okay fuck off!" I laughed. "We'll talk tomorrow."

"Bitch call me *tonight*, the fuck?" Kae fussed. "You think you too grown to check in when you get home?"

"It'll probably be *tomorrow* when gets home," Claire guessed. "And she's probably planning to spend the night with Calvin and his dick anyway."

The knock sounded again, a little firmer this time.

"Y'all make me sick – I'll check in, okay?" I promised, and they nodded.

"Okay my baby, have fun!"

"Yesss, have the best time!"

"I will! Love y'all, bye!"

Once the call was ended, I stood there for a moment, just to catch my breath before I grabbed my clutch and headed for the door.

Where I took *another* breath.

It's not a date.

It's not a date.

It's not a – damn.

I opened the door to find Calvin poised to knock again, looking *way*, way, better than expected.

Criminally fine, actually, in all black, diamond crusted chain around his neck, and a fresh lineup.

And he smelled *good.*

"Well *goddamn,*" was the first thing off his lips, and he looked away from me, shaking his head.

"What?!" I asked, alarmed, but he just shook his head again, taking a step back.

"Man... just bring your fine ass on before we don't even go to this shit," he said, already heading down the hall.

Oh.

Yeah.

I looked *good.*

Laughing, I locked my door and then caught up to him – which didn't take much, because he'd stopped to wait for me, with his hand extended.

I looked at it.

Looked at him.

Accepted his hand.

Is this a fucking date?

His hand was warm, secure around mine as he led me to the elevator and punched the button. It had been moving even slower than usual lately, so as we listened to it rumble down from a higher floor, Calvin had plenty of time to turn and give me a slow perusal that made me finally understand the term "hot in the ass" like my Mama used to say.

There was *definitely* some heat going on down there.

The elevator chimed.

The door crawled open.

And... there Hunter was.

Fuuuuck.

Every moment of realization was clear on his face – me being there. Me being there, with Calvin. Me being there, with Calvin, wearing *that* dress.

Calvin put a hand at the small of my back, ushering me into the steel box with my ex.

We stepped to the other side of where Hunter was standing… with the woman I'd seen him with at Urban Grind.

Both were staring.

From slightly behind me, Calvin's arm wrapped around my waist, pulling me into him with a possessive hand. His head dropped, lips grazing me on the neck, soft and deceptively possessive. "You good, baby?" he asked – low enough that it really was a private question, but not so low they couldn't hear it.

"Yeah," I answered, closing my eyes as his lips touched my neck again – this time, for a quick, purposeful kiss.

"Good."

I did *not* look up.

Didn't dare.

I could feel Hunter and his new supply looking at me, at us, as the elevator took its' sweet time delivering us to the ground floor, but I was *way* too interested in my pedicure to give them my attention.

"Have a good night," Calvin called after them when the elevator finally opened and they rushed off first.

"Thanks, you too," the woman replied, polite, as we followed them off.

Hunter just glared as he grabbed her hand to pull her outside.

"That was awkward," Calvin laughed once they were gone. "What do you think he's so pissed off about?"

"Kae told me you were his favorite player, so… that, probably," I explained. "Or, maybe you antagonizing him?"

"When did I do that?"

I sucked my teeth. "Calvin...that kiss? Calling me baby?"

"Oh that? I was just stepping into tonight's character."

"Is that right?"

"Yeah," he grinned, grabbing my hand to lead me outside. "Come on baby."

I didn't offer any pushback as he directed me to the black-on-black Range Rover I really should've already clocked as his, from the moment I noticed it in the apartment lot.

He led me to the passenger side, opened the door for me, helped me in, all that, and a few moments later, we were on our way.

"So, I was thinking," I said, eyeing him from the passenger seat – one hand on the wheel, the other on my leg, thumb tapping my thigh to the beat of the music.

He was very, very comfortable.

"Oh lord, here we go," he groaned, making my eyes go wide.

"Excuse me?"

"I'm fucking with you – what's up?" he asked, shooting me a grin.

I rolled my eyes.

"*Anyway*," I said, crossing my arms. "*I was thinking...* what's our storyline? Or rather... mine."

"Huh?"

"What you said about stepping into character – so, I know we decided to just keep it honest about how long we've "been together", which is fine. But, if I'm playing this role – stepping into character, like you said – I need a persona. I think that would make everything just kinda flow more naturally."

141

"You could just... be yourself?"

I scoffed. "I'm *myself* every day, and love her, real bad," I assured him. "But why not make this fun, and be... somebody else?"

He nodded. "Okay... I think I get it. What's your options?"

I shimmied in my seat, excited to have him indulging the idea. "Okay – option one, chaotic gold-digger baddie that's clearly only with you for a come up. And you know that, right? But my pussy is just too good, you're addicted to the drama, and I was down for you when you were in your suspended era."

"Suspended era is nuts."

"But accurate," I said. "Is that the only thing you heard?"

"Nah – but option one isn't gonna work. If my team at RSM gets even a *whiff* of that, Cole and Chloe will have your ass disappeared, and we don't want that."

My eyes went wide. "Definitely not. Okay – option two then. I'm a sweet angel baby, and we just fell in love at first sight, and can't wait to drop this whole career woman thing to have a whole team of kids after you make your comeback from your suspended era."

"Again with the sus—"

"Actually never mind, I don't think I could play that role all night without throwing up," I interrupted. So, scratch option two. Option *three*, I'm a no-nonsense, do *not* mess with my man, ready to throw hands kinda bitch. Again with the whole *you're addicted to this pussy* angle. And... I don't know shit about basketball, but I'll pretend for you... to support you through your suspended era."

"Literally *what* is it with the "suspended era" thing, what is that??"

"The *era* where your ass was not welcome on the field!"

"Field?!"

"Pitch, court, whatever!" I laughed. "You couldn't play for a period of time, also known as an era."

"Isn't it a pretty specific period length?"

"Colloquially, no," I answered with a smirk. "Anyway – I think we'll go with option three."

"Do *not* put your hands on anybody please."

"So you can fight but I can't?"

"Amelia…"

"What?!" I laughed. "Seriously – do you really think I need to be told to keep my hands to myself?"

He shrugged. "You're a little unpredictable, so…"

I fake gasped. "Me?! Excuse you, I am quite reliable and organized and things *consistently* go exactly as I planned them, for your information."

"Since *when*?!"

"Since *always!*" I countered. "I've just been having a difficult four to six weeks!"

"That is both too specific and *not* specific enough – why the range?"

"Well… I may or may not taken a little spill out of my chair the other day, and bumped my head the tiniest bit—"

"You're *concussed?!*"

My mouth dropped open. "*No!*" I denied.

"The other day… meaning a little while after I left from hanging that chair up?"

I shrugged. "That's such a subjective frame of reference—"

"I *heard* you fall, and texted you," he interrupted, pulling into a parking spot in front of a building in Black-

143

wood. "You acted like you didn't know what I was talking about!"

"I was *really* dazed."

"Amelia!"

"It wasn't that serious, relax."

His eyes went wide. "Relax? You just implied *memory loss* from falling out of that damn chair!"

"So you're the only one who can tell a joke now?"

He scoffed. "So you're a comedian?"

"Not *a* comedian – *your* comedian," I grinned. "I'm adding that to the personality for tonight."

"What the fuck have I done," he muttered, making me laugh as he climbed out of the car. A moment later, he was at my door, opening it to help me out... but not moving to give me any room. "Aye," he said, from very close to me, hand at my waist. "I'm down with fucking around to pass the time, clowning, all that, okay?" he said, before putting a finger under my chin, tipping my face up to his. "But whatever role you're stepping into... make sure there's no ambiguity."

"About what?" I breathed.

Barely.

Calvin stepped back, smirking as he laced our fingers. "About you being mine."

15 /
amelia

I *LOVED* a good reality TV moment.

The drama, the shade, the insane displays of wealth that were often harbingers of financial woes... messy, messy, messy.

Sucked for them, obviously, but great entertainment for me.

We'd only been there for maybe ten minutes when I got an introduction to one of his agents, Nicole Richardson, who I could *feel* the approval radiating off of.

It was a *great* note to start on, but then things started to whirl a little.

It was a *lot* of people, a lot of noise, just... a lot, honestly.

Calvin pulled me into a marginally quieter spot, his beard tickling my ear as he leaned in to ask if I was okay.

I smirked, and stepped away from him, planting an imaginary camera crew in my head and ready to break the fourth wall for my first confessional.

"Do you see this dress? Do you see how I *look* in this dress? Do you see everybody else seeing how I look in this dress? I'm in my element, okay?"

"Wait – am I the producer in this scenario?" Calvin asked, grinning.

"*Yes!*" I answered, excited that he'd immediately picked up on it.

"Heard you," he countered. "Okay... so you're in your element... not at all intimidated by the level of talent and fame in this room?"

"When everybody in the room has notoriety, it levels the playing field – why would I be—*Oh my God, is that Aurora Martin!*" I shrieked – *quietly* – immediately dropping my supposed reality TV game.

Rori Martin was an absolute inspiration for me – another Black woman in tech who'd built her app, Baby-Bee, into a massive success.

I'd *studied* her.

... the fact that she'd bagged two different professional athletes herself was purely coincidental.

"Yeah – she probably came with Tate," Calvin said, referencing the second of the athletes – the first was *not* worth mentioning. "You want to meet her?"

"What?" I asked, eyes wide. "No, this isn't... this isn't that type of thing, and I'm sure she doesn't want—"

"Nah, she's probably bored out of her mind," Calvin said, grabbing my hand to pull me along anyway.

Straight to where Rori was standing, with Sierra Ward.

I was going to pass the fuck out.

"Crossover Calllll," Sierra greeted him warmly, with a hug that let me know there was genuine love there.

"Hey Si-Si," he returned the greeting. "This is Li-Li."

"In front of people?!" was out of my mouth before I could help it, and my surprise at not being able to control my tongue must've been written all over my face, because the group laughed before I could fix it.

146

"My bad," Calvin said. "Sierra, this is Amelia."

"Hi Amelia," she gushed, grabbing my hand. "Calvin... she's gorgeous. Why haven't you brought her to the house?"

He shrugged. "I had to bargain and beg to get her out to this – she only came for the goodie bag, really."

Why would he say that?

"Cause he always thinks something is funny," Sierra answered, making me realize I'd said that out loud.

Fuck.

"Don't worry about it girlie – I'm just here for the gift bag too," Rori spoke up, and my heart moved from my throat to my ass and back as she extended a hand to me. "Aurora Martin."

"Are you kidding? I know who you are!" I squealed, excitedly accepting her hand.

So much for keeping my cool.

"Amelia Robbins," I told her, and her eyes went wide.

"From Proxy?"

Don't scream.

Don't scream.

Don't scream.

"You know who I am?!" I screamed, making her laugh.

"Well, I recognized the name – my team is supposed to be reaching out to you soon about a partnership opportunity for BabyBee. We're thinking a subsidized discount on diaper deliveries, arranging breastmilk donations, and so on."

"I *love* that," I gushed, then immediately tempered myself as I remembered *why* I was here.

I glanced at Calvin, who'd just been standing there quiet, half expecting him to look annoyed over this diversion from him. Instead, he looked kinda... *proud?*

He inclined his head, like he was prompting me to turn my attention back to Rori, which was enough encouragement for me to get right back to it. "We have to talk details."

"Absolutely," Rori said, squeezing my hand – *am I really holding hands with Rori Martin and Sierra Ward right now?!* "I'll have my people move that up the priority list since I know for sure that you're interested."

This is so much better than a gift bag.

"Glad you think so," Sierra laughed, and I didn't even have time to be embarrassed by that before someone else had walked up—a trio of men I soon realized were some of Calvin's Brawler teammates, boisterous and excited to see him.

It was so annoying.

But.

This wasn't about me, it was about him, so I was cool, especially knowing I was going to have that interaction with Rori to keep me warm at night for the rest of my life.

There were several more interactions like that – meeting Calvin's teammates, friends, and fans. I played my role in each one, knowing my only real requirement was being fine.

I was too overwhelmed to lean into my "character".

Especially when two – fine ass – men came up to Calvin to pull him aside after offering me a friendly greeting.

Their security made two things clear – they were *real* celebrities, and I was not part of whatever conversation they were having, leading me to believe these must be the team "superstars" – Kevion Ward and Thierry Baptiste.

All I knew is they were fine.

Matter of fact, damn near everybody here was, which

made Calvin's words about remembering I was his – for the night, at least – hold a little more weight. There were most certainly people here trying to choose and *be* chosen... which was the perfect backdrop to my next interaction.

Getting approached by a trio of ringless baddies who offered no ambiguity around them looking me up and down to size me up.

"Where did Cross find *you*?" one of them asked, prompting me to glance at where he was standing a few feet away, still engrossed in conversation.

I looked back at her with a smirk.

Rehab?

The strip club?

The maternity ward?

There were so many hilariously scandalous options I could go with, if I wanted to go with maximum trolling. But, because I didn't want to risk something that could wind up in the rumor mill, I went with—

"The clearance section," I answered, rolling my eyes.

"Yeah, we can tell," one of the friends chimed in, setting off giggles between them. "The dress?"

"Wait – is this... are y'all trying to... *bully me*?" I leaned in, whispering that last part in disbelief. "I really thought that was some TV shit, but y'all are *actually* about that life? *Wow*."

"What? Okay bitch you're weird," the third friend yapped.

I put a hand to my chest. "Y'all came over here to press me about *my* nigga and *I'm* weird? Okay," I said, looking around. "Where is the camera, actually? Did Calvin tell y'all to do this?"

"What?! Nobody told us to come talk to your ass!"

"*Sure*," I winked, still looking around for a camera, a boom mic, something. "I'm sorry to ruin the prank, but this is just... way too corny to not be scripted."

One of them sucked her teeth. "Let's just get away from this weird ass girl," one of the friends said, and they immediately saw their asses away from me.

Good.

Cause literally... *what*?

Of course I knew nobody planned that – they were just bitches.

Bitches who were either too stupid to realize what had just happened, or they would play the interaction in their head over and over, trying to figure out where their attempt to bully or intimidate me had gone wrong.

Either way, I won.

As they walked off, I caught eyes with Calvin. He gave me raised eyebrows that I interpreted as an unspoken check-in, so I nodded, offering a smile in return.

I wasn't really bothered by that encounter – I was exhilarated, actually.

I motioned Calvin back to his conversation, and saw my way to the open bar for a cute lemon drop, then found myself an empty seat.

To drink my cute lemon drop and mind my business.

Until... I heard Calvin's name.

Even though my ears perked up, I made a point of not looking in the direction the conversation was coming from immediately, turning on a level of nosiness Kae would've been proud of.

"I know man, that shit is wild – he must be fucking somebody in the front office too, cause ain't no way that got rid of a whole *coach* to accommodate this nigga."

"Right? And niggas talking about some damn *stats*. He got a MVP three damn years ago, and not again since then – he ain't *that* good."

That was the comment that made me feign something happening with my earring so I could glance behind me – I needed to see who was talking.

I know that ain't who I think it is.

My eyes narrowed, looking a little harder.

And it was, indeed, who I thought it was.

Two of the men who'd interrupted the conversation with Sierra and Rori to speak to Calvin.

The very ones who'd been grinning from ear to ear to get in his face – if I remembered correctly, they were his *teammates*.

Damn.

This is some real hater ass shit.

"What?"

"What?!" I repeated back, eyes wide.

Both men were looking straight at me, forcing me to come to the quick conclusion that my declaration about their behavior had been an outside thought instead of an inside one.

Oh.

Damn.

Anyway.

"Were you talking to us?" One of them asked, moving closer as he bit his lip.

I didn't even try to stop my nose from wrinkling up. "Why would I be talking to you, first of all," I said, standing from my seat – I did *not* feel comfortable with them towering over me. "With that said though… if the shoe fits…"

"Aye – mind your business, bitch," the other one said.

"Well you were talking about my man, so it kinda *is* my business... *bitch*," I countered... fully ready to run away screaming if I needed to.

Instead... I found myself face to face with Calvin, who had come out of absolutely nowhere.

"Did I forget to tell you to stay out of trouble?" he asked, smirking like there wasn't a nigga behind him looking like he wanted to smack me across the face. He grabbed my hand, fingers sliding between mine as he leaned into me. "I could *swear* we covered that."

"Yeah, control your bitch, man."

Immediately, any sense of amusement left Calvin's face, and he turned around, looking not at either of the men who'd been talking about him, but the third one that had been with them earlier, and just walked up. "Ay – you're my teammate, these are your guests. They're wilding right now. Control your bitches."

Oh.

Oh.

That was really, *really* nasty.

I *loved* it.

They... did not.

Calvin laughed as they immediately got irate – and immediately got removed by security before anything could really pop off.

"See how you almost got me into trouble?" he asked, shaking his head as he led me away. "This isn't supposed to be this kinda thing."

"But they were talking shit about you!" I defended myself, and Calvin smirked.

"Oh, so you were protecting me? I'm honored," he laughed. "Next time could you do it in a way that won't mean I've gotta beat somebody up?"

"But... I *want* to see you beat somebody up. It would be good for the show."

"The show? You're damn fool," he chuckled, slipping hands around my waist to pull me close – there was music going, and I quickly realized he'd led me to a dance floor.

I grinned. "You like it."

"I do, actually. We almost had to cut the cameras. Still might," he flirted, with an exaggerate eyebrow wag I couldn't do anything *but* laugh at.

Even after such heavy tension, just a moment ago, he had me right back in the best of moods, so, *so* easily.

It was honestly crazy.

I found myself grooving with him – having a blast, actually, for another half hour before he leaned in again.

"Let's get you of here."

My eyes went wide. "Seriously?" I asked. "Isn't it a little early? Did I get us in trouble?"

"Man, I've successfully showed my face at this shit and now I'm ready to go," he answered. "A little bit because of you. Just a little though."

I gasped. "What'd I do?!"

"What *didn't* you?!" he laughed as he led me back out front to approach the valet.

A very familiar looking valet, who licked her lips, rubbing her hands together as soon she saw me. "Amanda, right? You looking real good. *Real* good," Jeanie said, fully ignoring Calvin.

"Right in front of me? This is some bullshit," he said, prompting Jeanie to shoot him a scowl.

"Sir, I'm trying to have a conversation if you don't mind," she said.

He scoffed. "I *do* mind. What's your pronouns?"

Her eyebrows went up. "You know – thank you for being respectful. Primarily, she and her, but really I'm good with any. I'm a very fluid individual."

"Right, right," Calvin grinned. "Miss Nigga, can you go get my shit and stop trying to press my girl in my face please?"

She put a hand to her chest. "That is *so* disrespectful!"

"How?" Calvin questioned.

"I ain't figured it out yet, but as soon as I do, you're getting cancelled, nigga."

"Cool – in the meantime, it's the black on black Range."

"You and every other unoriginal ass athlete in this bitch, I'ma need more information than that."

"Jeanie! You *cannot* talk to the clients like that!"

We all looked back to find a white woman with an asymmetrical bob and a blazer with the valet company logo embroidered on the lapel standing close by, looking scandalized.

"Ah hell, I can't lose another job. My ol' lady gone put me out for real this time," Jeanie groaned, and Calvin blew out a sigh.

"Ay – we're all cool ma'am, just banter between friends – we'll keep it more professional moving forward," Calvin told the woman – clearly the manager – who gave a stiff nod before shooting Jeanie another warning glare.

"Good looking out," Jeanie said, once the coast was clear. "Amanda – you keep good company, I like that."

"Amelia."

"Who the fuck is that?" Jeanie asked, already walking off. "Let me go get this lil wack ass Range Rover."

"Why my shit gotta be *wack*?!" Calvin called after her,

then looked at me. "See what I mean? Trouble, wherever you go."

I gasped. "How is this on me?!"

Calvin smirked, grabbing my hand to pull me closer. "Isn't it always?"

16 /
amelia

"So... how do you think I did tonight?" I asked, halfway through the drive back to the Heights.

Calvin glanced at me, grinning before he put his eyes back on the road. "You want like... a grade?"

"Duh," I answered. "Do I *not* seem like someone who thrives on validation?"

He laughed. "Good point. Uh... Let me see... you definitely lost points for me having to call somebody a bitch on your behalf."

I scoffed. "Hey – the designation of bitches has been equally distributed tonight – that word got a used a *lot*. In *your* defense – they were talking shit about you!"

"You know... that's fair. You should actually *get* points for that. But... to be clear, those niggas were plus-ones for somebody who is practice team *at best*. Nobody was sweating them, and you shouldn't either."

"It was just a little too fake for me – they literally interrupted us to dick ride, just to turn around and hate," I whined, crossing my arms. "I don't like that."

"Who does?" he laughed. "It's just... life, you know?

157

Don't let it bother you. I appreciate you holding me down though."

"Aw. That's what I was there for, babe," I replied, tagging on a little kissy-face expression for extra seasoning.

"Babe?"

"I called you that as my character – don't get excited."

"Too late," he quipped. "You've given me an opening."

"It's a trap, actually -- I'm waiting with a bat for you to walk through."

"Damn," Calvin laughed. "You're talking like it would be *so bad* to fuck with me – you think I'd be a bad boyfriend or something?"

"I think it could go either way, actually," I admitted. "Extremes, though."

"Huh?"

"You're either an *excellent* boyfriend, or someone's *did I tell you how I almost ended up in jail for killing this nigga* story. No in-between."

"That's intense," he chuckled. "How can you make that judgement before you even know what's in the benefit package?"

"Benefit package? Is that like my – wait, I didn't get my gift bag!" I fussed, realizing my –supposed—primary reason for attending this little shindig was indeed *not* in my possession.

"Oh, shit – I'll make sure you get it," Calvin said. "Because I'm what? An *excellent* boyfriend," he answered his own question. "The fuck you think this is?"

"Some bullshit," I replied. "An excellent boyfriend wouldn't have let me leave without it."

"Correction – an excellent boyfriend is human, and

therefore makes the occasional mistake. The true showing of merit comes from how he pivots – but your last nigga was wack, so you probably don't know anything about that."

"Uh, *ouch*," I scoffed, frowning at him. "That's actually a little offensive."

"My bad, baby," he said, reaching to grab my thigh. "How can I make it up to you?"

Immediately, my chest felt hot. "Baby?"

He grinned. "I can't be in character too? You don't like my method acting?"

His hand was still on my thigh.

Gripping.

My gaze skirted up to his. "I'm not sure that's what's happening, but... sure?"

"You're a hater, damn."

The rest of the ride was spent bantering back and forth, and I still had a grin on my face as he helped me out of the car in the building parking lot. All the way to our hall, in fact.

"Wow – you're not going to walk me to my door?" I asked, surprised when he stopped at his.

"I've got something for you real quick."

"You're not still in character are you?"

"Should I be?" he asked, wagging his eyebrows as he unlocked his door and stepped inside, clearly intending for me to follow.

So... I did.

As many times as he'd been in *my* apartment, I'd never been in his.

It was less... bachelor-y than I expected.

There wasn't anything gray in sight – it was domi-nated by warm wood tones and a surprising amount of plants. There were touches of orange and black – tasteful nods to his team colors that wouldn't necessarily register as out of place with the rest of the palette.

And it was *clean*.

Nice.

"Here," Calvin said, and I turned to find him extending a gift bag in my direction.

"This is from the party?" I asked, confused as I accepted it.

It was *heavy*.

"Nah," he said. "This is a little *thank you* for doing me this solid tonight."

Eyebrow raised, I took it to the counter and peeked into the bag, gasping a little as I pulled the tissue aside. "Now how in the world did you know I would love this?" I asked, pulling out a bottle of an ultra-bougie, artisanal version of my favorite cocktail mixer.

"That night on the balcony," he answered. "Remember, you picked the pineapple lemonade flavor, cause you thought it might be similar to a lemon drop. So when I saw a bottle at Nectar, I thought about you... figured you might like it."

I grinned. "You figured *very* right," I told him. "In fact... the lemon drop I was having when I heard those niggas hating... I did not get to enjoy it properly. Tell me you have vodka."

"I do."

"Then... let's drink," I suggested, already cracking the seal on the bottle.

"Bet," Calvin agreed, already moving for his liquor cabinet. Ten minutes later, we were perched on the couch with our drinks – I'd run next door to switch out of my dress into lounge clothes, and when I came back, he'd already done the same.

"This is *nuts*," I groaned after I'd taken a first sip. It was the perfect blend our sour and sweet, the vodka was smooth, the citrus was vibrant... "you did your biggest with this one. Thank you."

"Thank *you*," he countered. "Like I said – I appreciate you being Team Calvin, even if it's just for one night."

I started to respond to that, but my phone chimed – a quick glance told me it was Kae.

Sending a picture.

Frowning, I navigated to the message to find that it was a screenshot... from some gossip account on social media, with a picture of me and Calvin.

"So it begins," I said, holding up the phone to show him the image. "Good thing we kinda expected this, right?"

He nodded, taking a sip from his drink. "Yeah, we knew it was coming... it's not going to make any trouble for you, right?"

"Trouble with who? I'm grown," I laughed. "And *very* single."

"So we broke up?"

I raised an eyebrow. "Huh?"

"You said *very* single," he explained, leaning forward. "like you really needed it emphasized that you're a free woman, and I'm just trying to understand when that happened. I thought we were in character?"

"Even now?"

"Why not?" he shrugged. "I mean... drinking together in our socks is definitely a kind of intimacy, if you ask me."

"Friendly intimacy, I thought."

He nodded a little, then sat back. "Message received."

"Who said I was sending a message?" I asked. "I'm just giving you my honest thoughts."

"And what are you thinking right now, honestly?"

"Honestly?"

"Yeah," he chuckled. "*Honestly.*"

I bit down on my lip, surveying him for a moment as I considered my answer. And then...

"Honestly... this vodka is making me feel like I want to climb in your lap."

His eyebrows went up. "What's stopping you?"

"Relationship status." I put my empty glass down on the table, focusing on Calvin's face. "I enjoy being able to enjoy your company without it being some weird thing."

"It doesn't have to be anything we don't make it."

"Yeah, people say that shit all the time and then end up in a situationship that wrecks their mental health and turns them into a relationship super-villain for the next poor sucker who has the misfortune of crossing paths with them."

"Damn."

I laughed. "I mean... I've seen it a million times. And I don't want that for myself – or you."

"I don't want that for either of us either... and... you have sufficiently spooked me out of getting involved with anything that resembles what you're talking about."

"Which is a shame," I sighed. "Cause I really, *really* want to sit on your dick."

I kinda hated how easy it was for me to admit out loud, knowing I wasn't supposed to be on that type of timing.

But... there it was.

He choked a little on the last of his drink. "That... escalated."

"Vodka kicked in a little more," I admitted, already moving... to get into his lap.

He offered no objection to my completely contradictory actions, just teased me with a *"blame it on the alcohol"* reference, then grabbed *immediate* handfuls of ass once he'd practically tossed his finished drink on the table.

"Now what?" he asked.

Was it the alcohol?

Or was this really always as inevitable as the electricity I felt between us right now suggested, and I was simply... giving in to it.

Again.

Finally.

I shifted a little – the fabric layers between us were very thin, and did little to cushion anything. I felt exactly how hard he was, felt the tension in his arms, easily clocked the restraint in his eyes.

"Promise me you won't be weird after this."

He scoffed. "If memory serves, *you* were the one being weird last time."

"I have no idea what you're talking about."

"Right," he chuckled, and then one of his hands left my ass to cuff the back of my head, pulling my mouth down to his for a greedy kiss I eagerly obliged.

It felt so... *easy.*

Or maybe... *natural* was the better word.

Those hands were everywhere – gripping, guiding as he stood me up, sliding my shorts and panties down my hips. Tossing my clothes to the floor, teasing me with his fingers on my clit. Pulling me back to my knees on the couch with him, putting one of my legs over his shoulder. Spreading me open, sinking those fingers into me.

And his mouth... very, very busy as well.

Slow, long, careful licks along my inner thighs, little nips with his teeth that he soothed with soft kisses while his fingers worked, while he made me make a mess. One of my hands gripped the couch, the other gripped his hair for balance as he kissed, nipped, licked his way to my clit, covering it with his mouth, lapping with his tongue as his fingers *still* worked.

I came so hard I saw stars, practically collapsing over the back of the couch if he hadn't caught me, laughing.

He stopped laughing when I deftly snatched his dick out of his boxers, sinking down onto it.

"What's funny?" I whispered against his lips as I flexed around him, reflexively pulling him deeper into me.

"Not a damn thing?" was his shaky reply.

I grinned... then sank my knees deeper into his couch for stability.

Then I did what I had really, *really* been wanting to do for weeks now.

I rode the fuck outta him.

I had just enough miles on my knees to get us both to a climax, and then I just didn't move – I wasn't worried about him pulling out because my birth control was iron clad.

Calvin's hands were still on my hips – soft at first, but then suddenly firm as he lifted me off him, depositing me on the couch.

Very, very briefly, I felt a little.... I don't know.

Bereft?

Offended?

Whatever it was, it only lasted long enough for him to stand up, gather his footing, and scoop me into his arms.

"*Ah!*" I shrieked, taken off guard by the sudden movement. "What's happening?" I asked.

"We're washing up," he explained. "And then I'm getting my lick back."

I grinned. "Lick back?"

"Yeah. You didn't think I was letting you leave after fucking me like that, right?"

17 /
calvin

"You sure you don't have anything better to do? No woman to be laid up with or something? Damn!" I shot at Arthur, sick of hearing his mouth, honestly.

I'd come outside at the asscrack of dawn to shoot around so I could clear my head – I'd even grabbed the overpriced "silent" ball to avoid annoying the neighborhood, or *attracting attention.*

And yet and still.

There Arthur was, on the stoop, *Arthur's Fine Flooring* hat pulled back off his face like Elmer Fudd.

Mouth *running.*

"You talking about me not having a woman to lay up under like you not out here avoiding yours," he quipped.

"I'm not avoiding *her.*"

"So you *do* have somebody up there – I knew it!" he hooted.

Hollered.

All that shit, like it wasn't barely six in the morning.

Tuning him out, I went back to what I was doing – which *wasn't* avoiding Amelia, who as far as I knew, was still snoozing away in my bed after several rounds of pretending our relationship was something it wasn't.

Lazy, comfortable, relationship-type fucking, that clearly I'd done very well, since she hadn't rushed off. I... liked that.

I was looking forward to – or rather, hoping it was what I would find – her still being there when I got back upstairs.

My avoidance was firmly tuned on the impending start of the basketball season.

Was I *actually* ready?

Enough to be part of the team, of course.

Enough to step back into my place on the starting roster?

That... was a little less certain.

And it was hard to even figure out on my own – I hadn't been in a team practice, had been avoiding highlights of the games I missed. Two things that were changing very, very soon.

I didn't want to end up disappointed.

Didn't want to disappoint anyone, actually, myself included.

So... I kept at exactly what I'd been doing.

Drills.

Conditioning.

Shooting.

"You think you can get me some courtside seats?" Arthur asked, from suddenly way closer than he'd been when I first tuned him out.

Maybe too successfully, since he'd left the stoop to hobble his way on the court, causing me to way overshoot, landing my ball in the trash enclosure.

"Right up next to Sierra Ward's ol' pretty chocolate

self," Arthur kept talking. "You think that boy doing right by her? Cause if he not, I—"

"Could you not?!" I asked, shaking my head as I jogged over to the enclosure.

Luckily trash had just been picked up a day or so ago, so it wasn't too overrun with nastiness. I spotted the ball amongst a pile of boxes somebody had tossed into the area without breaking them down, maybe calling themselves leaving them for someone who needed them.

As I bent to grab the ball, a little flash of orange caught my attention. Curious, I flipped open the top of one of the boxes to see I was right – there was Brawlers' basketball stuff in the box – a box *full*, in fact.

Including a jersey.

A Calvin Cross jersey.

"Well damn, what they say fuck me for?!" I asked out loud, chuckling as I flipped the lid back closed. I was still shaking my head as I left the enclosure, ball tucked under my arm, mind running with possibilities for what the hell *that* was about.

"Ay," Arthur called as I stepped out of the enclosure. "You'll never guess what I seen last night!"

I sighed. "What?"

"Guess!"

"No," I refused, shaking my head as I went back to what I'd been doing before his interruption.

"That weird dude from upstairs—"

"I can think of five people that describes."

"The one used to deal with that pretty girl from next door to you."

I lowered the ball, eyes narrowed.

He had my attention now.

"What about him?" I asked.

"I seen him making a haul down to the garbage cans. All kinda mumbling, cussing under his breath. Boy he was *madder than a motherfucker,*" Arthur cackled. "Big ass box – dropped it halfway across the yard, spilled all his shit out."

"Eventually you're going to get to the point, right?"

"It was full of *Crossover* shit – boy you must've really hurt that nigga feelings, I'm telling you!"

"He doesn't even *know* me," I defended, even as my mind drifted back to last night... making a point of kissing on Amelia in the elevator.

Okay.

Fine.

Maybe I *was* antagonizing him.

But to put all that shit in a box in the trash instead of selling it was...

Damn.

He was *really* mad.

Oh well.

Sucks for him.

I... should probably stop fucking with him before he crashed out though.

Amelia *did* say he'd been a fan, and that first interaction in the elevator... he'd mentioned being excited to see me back on the court.

I was guessing that was no longer the case.

Hopefully throwing my shit away was the closure he needed, and there wouldn't be any more knocking at Amelia's door, cause I was going to *have* to beat his ass at that point.

Which was *exactly* the kinda problem I didn't need – especially considering the way the last messy ex situation had turned out for me.

Which... damn... it begged the question of... did I need *any* situation at all, going into training camp? This time needed to be focused, needed to be distraction-free.

Pissed-off exes were known for pulling attention.

On the *other* hand though... pretending I didn't like Amelia at this point would just be silly.

She was literally in my bed, afterall.

"Don't you worry about it," Arthur said, clapping a hand on my shoulder. "You got security money, right?"

I frowned. "Security? What the hell would I need security for? You heard something? Know something I don't know?"

"Just saying – niggas get crazy."

"So then, no," I laughed. "His feelings are just a little hurt, he'll be aiight."

I was saying it to get Arthur off my back about it, but I also fully believed it to be the case. I *certainly* wasn't about to be walking around the building looking over my shoulder... for the few days I had left before I would be relocating to Blackwood for training.

Hm.

I... felt like me and Amelia needed to have a little conversation.

Or... shit... was I overthinking last night?

It was kinda hard not to, with a shift from us becoming actual, honest friends to... whatever last night made us.

If it made us anything other than what we were already were.

I thrived on clarity, though.

I scooped up my ball, tucked it under my arm, and headed back up to my apartment, halfway wondering if she would even still be there.

She was.

Although, she'd clearly been up for a bit – fresh clothes, hair brushed, drinking coffee from a mug I'd never seen before in my life, all which led me to believe she'd probably gone home at some point to pull herself together.

"Damn, so you just left my shit wide open, huh?" I asked, prompting wide eyes from her.

"Not *wide open*," she defended. "But yes... unlocked. Only for like ten minutes though."

"Tell me anything," I grumbled, ambling over to where she was sitting at my kitchen counter. I walked right up to her... waited... she tipped her head back... looked at me.

Smiled.

And the crowd went *wild.*

In my head, at least.

Externally, I leaned down, planting a quick kiss against her lips... that immediately sent a look of confusion over her face.

"What was *that* for?!" she asked, clearly alarmed, clutching her coffee to her chest. "We ain't *never* did that before!"

Well damn.

Her pulling back like that was... *damn.*

"I could draw your vulva from memory at this point Amelia, what do you mean?" I challenged, not understanding why she was still putting distance between us.

She scowled at me. "I *mean*, that kiss was like... that wasn't... that felt different. Why did you do that?"

"Is that not what you wanted me to do?!"

"What would make you think that?!"

"You tipped your head back!"

"*You're tall!*"

"I…" I shook my head, chuckling as I let the ball roll into the corner where I usually left it. "Clearly this was a miscommunication… but it answers a lot of questions I had."

"No, no, no," Amelia denied, putting her cup down. "You haven't asked anything, so let's not do that. If we have questions, we should ask them straight out, not make assumptions."

"That only works if we're gonna be honest."

"Okay," she shrugged. "So let's be honest."

"Do you have a problem with me kissing you?" I asked, and her eyes went wide like she was surprised I'd just gotten straight to the point.

"No," she answered. "It just caught me off guard, because I associate a kiss like that with… a certain level of intimacy."

"More intimate than we've been?"

"*Different* intimate than we've been," she replied. "Or… maybe not so much, actually. Considering… everything."

"What does that mean?"

She sighed. "It means… I think we have taken this friendship to the boundary of something else."

"Is that a bad thing?"

"It's… I don't know that it's a healthy thing for me. But it feels too natural to be *bad*. I think."

"Natural?"

"As in…coming very easily," she explained. "Surely you've noticed the same?"

"You mean, how we vibe with each other? Yeah. Of course."

"Okay. So... I guess... what does this mean? Does it mean something?"

"Are you asking me what we are?"

She sucked her teeth. "Uh-uh – do *not* lay the burden of that on my feet," she said. "I told you already – I'm not far enough removed from the breakup with Hunter for... any of this, actually. And yet, here we are. I don't have to pretend to not have feelings for you, but I'm *not* going to be the one pushing for us to define something."

"I don't think we have to *define* anything – I don't know that we *should*, actually. I'm just... I know there's something here, and I know I'm getting ready to spend time in Blackwood, so I'm not going to be around. So... I didn't know if it was going to be weird – if you were going to feel... shit, I don't know."

This was... not the type of conversation I found myself in, not really.

I'd had a couple of serious relationships as an adult, but they had all followed a more clear path – attraction, intimacy, conversation, couple.

Until one of those conversations revealed the inevitable deal breaker.

Then, trying to make it work anyway, until it just has to be called what it is – *over*.

Never... whatever this was.

Never this... *natural*.

"Calvin," Amelia smiled. "Were you wondering if I was going to miss you?"

I shrugged. "I'on know. I mean... yeah, maybe a little."

"Of course I'm going to miss you."

Straight like that.

Soft, and certain, hitting me right under the ribs.

Like it was the most obvious thing in the world.

I suppressed my grin – tried to, at least.

"I can't get a *same* or something?!" Amelia huffed, eyebrow raised, making me laugh.

"Come on now," I said, closing the distance I'd put between us after she reacted like she did to the kiss. "That's not really a question, is it?"

"That is *not* a yes."

"Yes, Amelia, damn. I will miss you. Is that what you want to hear?"

"Nigga. You are not Martin, and I'm not Gina, do *not* play with me right now."

"You not feeling the reference right now?"

She shook her head. "Absolutely not – we're having a very serious, very awkward conversation right now. I need you to lock in."

"Bet. So... what's the verdict?" I asked. "What's our conclusion here?"

Amelia shrugged. "I... don't know. I don't want to not call a thing a thing, but... I'm not ready to call it a thing."

"So we won't then," I said. "We'll just... vibe."

She looked at me for a moment, then nodded. "Yeah. We'll vibe."

18 /
amelia

I NEVER SHOULD'VE ADMITTED I was going to miss him.

It gave him *way* too much power.

In the days since that conversation, he'd been even *more* confident, funnier, sexier, *better in bed.*

Not that I should know that last one, but... whatever.

We were grown.

And I was, *way* too quickly, approaching gone in the head.

Dangerous, when we'd very distinctly decided to *not* define... this.

"Babe – you good?" Calvin asked, pulling my attention from a display of heirloom tomatoes at *Fresh*. I didn't even need tomatoes, but I grabbed a couple anyway, trying to cover the fact that I was zoned out.

"Yeah – these are gorgeous, right?"

I held up the tomatoes, ready to put them in the cart – top tier was mine, while he was using the bottom – but my smile must've been a little too plastered on.

Calvin's eyes narrowed, and then he grinned at me. "Yeah – they're nice. Whatcha thinkin' about?"

The fact that you're about to return to your "real" life as a professional athlete, with a demanding schedule, competitive stress, physical demands, insane travel, cameras and mics in your face, and women throwing themselves at you.

"A pizza, maybe?" I answered, putting the tomatoes in a little basket in the cart. "A few weeks ago, I had one what was heirloom tomato, basil, mozzarella – like a caprese pizza. Or would that just be a margherita?"

"Now you know damn well that's not what I'm asking you," he chuckled. "Seriously – what's on your mind?"

"Mistakes."

His eyebrow went up. "Elaborate."

"No thank you."

"You can't say some cryptic shit like that and then just not address it."

"Watch me," I countered with a shrug, trying to walk away.

Calvin easily caught me though, anchoring a hand on either side of me with my back to the cart.

Basically pinning me against it, triggering my heart to start racing.

Nowhere to go, nothing to do except... face it.

"You think we're a mistake?" he asked.

"I think I was supposed to be like... healing, or something. Not having quiet domestic moments like this with *you*," I answered.

"So you think we're a mistake."

"I didn't say that."

"It's being implied."

"Not intentionally."

"Oh, so this is accidental sabotage, then."

I sucked my teeth, looking away, but he quickly grabbed me under the chin, bringing my face back to his.

"I understand that you are still hurting from your

last relationship, which makes this timing less than ideal. I get it, I swear. Okay?" he insisted. "If you want us to just put a pin in this, see what's up after the season is over, whatever, we can do that. But what did we say?"

I sighed. "We said we would vibe."

"What are you absolutely *not* doing right now?"

"Vibing," I huffed, rolling my eyes. "But *not* for lack of trying."

"What's stopping you?"

"*Reality*," I groaned. "All the possibilities about all the ways this could go *so* utterly wrong."

"So you're gonna beat fate and fuck it up early?"

"You can't *beat* fate," I scoffed.

"Exactly." He leaned in, pressing his lips to my forehead.

Lingering.

It was so, *so* good.

I was going to implode.

"Li-Li," he muttered, still close enough that his lips were brushing my skin. "You *can't* beat fate... so you may as well vibe."

"You make it sound so easy."

"Because it is," he countered. "Now... what else do we need for the pizza you mentioned? Oh, and didn't you talk about getting cucumbers?"

"None from here – my mom is bringing some in a few days," I answered. "As far as the pizza, uh... there should be some fresh mozzarella in the coolers inside."

And just like that, I was successfully redirected.

I was – we were – *vibing*.

I'd be lying if I didn't admit that seeing his suitcase packed, sitting by his door, and helping him clear the

179

perishables from his fridge didn't bring back my panicky feelings.

It was crazy to start up a *thing* right before one of the people was going to be out of pocket for weeks, right? I mean, sure – Blackwood was twenty minutes up the road, forty with heavy traffic, so it wasn't like he was going to the other side of the world, but still.

He was going to be busy – getting his spot back on the team, reacclimating to athlete mode – late nights and early mornings, physical strain.

And *stress*.

I know this shit had to be stressful.

On the outside, it didn't show – he was upbeat, cracking jokes, flirting, all his usual stuff. His friend from the hardware store, Marquis came by, with a wood-fired pizza oven strapped to the back of a huge pickup. Him, Calvin, and a another guy he'd brought along – Foster, apparently – got it down off the truck with Arthur, who'd materialized from nowhere in an *Arthur's Outdoors and More* hat supervising while they set it up in the courtyard with the grills.

Because I *very* casually mentioned that I thought the pizzas would be better in a "real" pizza oven.

Hands propped at his sides, Calvin looked at me with a grin. "Okay – you read to make some pizza now?"

"Oh… you thought I meant… *today*?" I asked, keeping the confused look on my face as his smile melted away. He looked at the pizza oven, then back at me, then at his friends who were still panting from the late-summer heat and effort they'd just put into setting that thing up.

"Are you… deadass?" he asked, completely serious.

Then I smiled.

"Just fucking with you."

I couldn't name a better feeling than his friends – and Arthur – busting out laughing as he nodded, then started clapping.

"You got me good with that one – I legit felt a tear forming," he laughed, pulling me into a hug with his arm around my neck.

"Ay- y'all talking about pizza, but is it *not* a perfect day to put something on one of these *grills*?" Keys asked.

"Nigga... nobody put you keeps a rack of ribs at the ready *but* you," Foster chuckled. "You been looking for an opening all week haven't you?"

Keys sighed. "Man, I got banned from the corner store, and have had to suffer through the smell without any relief. Can you blame me?"

"Uh- *how* exactly does one get banned from there?" I asked. "Mrs. Spencer is literally the sweetest lady on the planet. Were you in there bothering her?!"

"Nahhh!" Keys defended. "That was my daddy's lil' sweetheart... until he fucked it up and she said she don't want nothing to do with the Coopers."

"Damn. Banned your whole bloodline?" Calvin asked, and Keys nodded. "That's tough."

"Agreed," Keys said. "So... im'a go grab these ribs and some charcoal then." He motioned for Foster to join him back in the truck as we laughed.

And... from there, it kinda... turned into a going-away party.

"You remember that night we met?" Calvin asked me, hours later, sitting at one of the benches in the courtyard while people talked, played, and ate around us. Some were neighbors, some were friends we'd called, some were people I'd never seen before in my life, which... was fine too, honestly.

We were vibing.

"How could I forget – the first time you ever trolled me," I laughed, leaning into his shoulder.

"You were mean as hell, in my defense."

"I was heartbroken, in *my* defense," I countered, eyebrow raised.

"Shit... me too," he said, making my eyebrows go even higher.

"Elaborate."

"Do you know what Summer League is?" he asked, and I immediately frowned.

"Do I *seem* like I would?"

Calvin chuckled. "No, actually. So, it's basically like... I'm sure you have some kind of orientation for Proxy, right? Like a trial run to make sure new people fit in whatever lane they're trying to get into, right?"

"Yeah."

"So that's kinda what Summer League is – making sure the rookies and other relatively new players can handle the heat, give them a chance to get play time they usually wouldn't, all that."

I nodded. "Okay, I follow. What about it though?"

"It's kinda... fuck it, it's some sensitive shit, I know. But, this one guy, not even on my team, mind you – he's on fire. Putting up impressive numbers, great personality, nigga is handsome, everything," he laughed. "Which usually, who gives a fuck, right? But I'm watching highlights, enjoying it even though it's bittersweet, and one of the damn announcers says, *"Crossover who?"* which, that's a basketball term, so it could've just been like... coincidence. But... *nah.* He goes on theis long tirade about how this other nigga is my replacement in the league, blah, blah, blah."

"Aww, did that hurt your feelings?" I asked, grabbing his hand.

"As a matter of fact, *yes*," he chuckled. "Like a motherfucker."

Ugh.

Hearing that needled at me, making me mad at a complete stranger. "Okay *fuck him*," I said, frowning. "Clearly, he didn't know what he was talking about, because you're on the team, reporting to training camp tomorrow, people clearly love you. What is his name?"

"Cool it, Li-Li," he said, squeezing my hand. "It's okay."

"Well yeah, but I still don't like it."

Shit, I didn't either. Keys and Foster were over here when it happened, and they immediately clocked the shift in my mood. Ordered some drinks – through Proxy, actually – invited some people... turned it into a get-together. Which had cheered me up until your mean ass came along."

I gasped, pushing him away. "That's not funny!"

"I'm not joking!" he insisted. "That shit blew me."

"So you decided to troll?"

He shrugged. "Just a little."

"A little? I wanted to murder you!"

"But you didn't, and look at how things have turned out."

I wrinkled my nose at him. "Are you implying that sleeping with you is my reward for not wringing your neck?"

"Hey... you said it, not me," he declared, sitting back with a cocky grin that made me roll my eyes.

Before I could formulate an actual reply though, Keys and Foster walked up, needling Calvin into hitting the court with them and some kids from the neighborhood who'd recognized him.

"Don't tear your Achilles!" I yelled after him, grinning as he responded with a wide eyed, *now why the fuck would you say that?!*

I could troll too.

Eventually, the impromptu party thinned out, with the last of the guests helping with the cleanup. Which... man, was a bit of a double-edged sword, because it took away the distraction of busyness, forcing me to sit with my frustratingly complicated feelings.

Alone.

I snuck back to my apartment while Arthur and Calvin were fussing about the pizza oven, which needed to be completely cool before it could be moved. I took a shower, then dressed for bed, hitting my group chat with Kae and Claire in between.

I absolutely needed them to be real with me.

"Babe... you need to be real with yourself. – Kae"

"Yeahhhhh... that's your man, sis. – Claire."

I tossed the phone down on the bed and stared up at the ceiling.

As soon as I closed my eyes, a knock sounded at the door.

I was up immediately, already knowing who I was going to find on the other side.

"I really thought we were better than this, Li-Li," Calvin said, breezing past me to come inside. "I can't believe you left me outside to argue with Arthur."

"My bad," I laughed. "I was trying to avoid an awkward moment."

"Of saying goodnight?"

"Of saying *goodbye*," I corrected. "Aren't you headed

to Blackwood super early in the morning? We won't see each other again before you leave."

"So you opted to just... not?"

"I never said it was a *good* plan."

Calvin shook his head, chuckling as he grabbed me around the waist to pull me close. "Stop being a—"

"Do *not* call me a weirdo," I warned, laughing when he pressed his lips to mine.

"You're doing your best impression of one though, how can I not?"

"I'm not trying to be weird, I'm trying to do what too many people avoid – process my feelings, instead of ignoring them, if that's okay."

His eyebrows went up. "you know what... fair point. Niggas do be *going with the flow* right into some bullshit."

"Exactly," I agreed. "And not even on any... *you're paying for the last man's mistakes* kinda stuff, just... being careful. So if I get a little quiet, or withdraw, it's not because I'm *not vibing*. I'm just assessing."

"And what am I doing while you're assessing?" he asked.

"Giving me a little patience, and grace, and knowing that I will never leave you in limbo about where I stand. You'll never have to wonder."

He nodded. "And I... can offer the same. Deal?"

"Deal."

"Good," he said. "Now... bring your ass on and give me a proper send off."

19 /
calvin

TWO-A-DAYS WERE SUPPOSED TO BUILD.

Endurance, strength, character, plus some other traits I was too exhausted to even pull to mind.

Because actually, the two-a-days were beating the shit out of me.

For all my conditioning and preparing and supposedly staying ready so I didn't have to get there... man.

The workouts, the drills, the shooting practices, the mock two-on-two scrimmages... *shit.* I guess I was glad I hadn't been just sitting around on my ass during my suspension, but for the strain training camp was putting on me, for the effort I was having to put into something that used to feel effortless... that *felt* like exactly what I'd been doing.

My legs may as well have been on somebody else's body for as much control I had over them as I collapsed onto a bench in the locker room, spent after a round of suicide drills.

"You're halfway through hell week," one of the trainers gleefully announced as he walked around handing out protein shakes. I couldn't even find the energy for a pissy look, let alone a snide remark, so I just took my shake and sat back to drain it with the provided straw while sweat dripped off me.

"Hell" week might be understating it, honestly.

Around me, rookies and other vets were in various states of exhaustion were going through the ritual – protein shake, shower, recovery if needed, and then finally home.

Just to be up at six to do the whole thing over again the next day.

At least no one would be able to claim a lack of readiness when it was time to get on the plane for the first game of the season in what *felt* like just a few days. We hadn't won the fuck of the draw with that one, on multiple fronts – we were headed to Tennessee to play the Trojans, which was *never* an easy game.

Assuming I actually got to play.

So far… I felt like my chances were looking good.

Thierry plopped down on the bench next to me with a groan, stretching his legs. "Cross… I thought you were fucking around when you said you'd been staying in shape. I feel bad for doubting you."

"Nigga… no you don't" I chuckled, almost choking on my shake. "Do you think I didn't hear you telling coach I didn't look tired?"

"Just trying to give you more opportunities to prove yourself."

"More favors is the last thing his ass needs," Jay muttered as he passed by, and it took everything in me to simply ignore that shit – I didn't need whatever drama he was on.

Especially since he'd been trying me all week, presumably still salty about the situation at the mixer between Amelia and his guests.

I *needed* my coaches to see I was capable of controlling myself.

"Man shut yo' bitch ass up," Thierry quipped – clearly uninterested in proving his self control.

He was a *known* crash-out, but also arguably one of the best centers in the league.

He had that kind of leverage.

"Kids – do I have to put somebody in timeout?" Kevion said as he stepped into the are, with a particularly pointed look at Jay, who was the one starting shit.

Jay just grunted, and went back to minding his own fucking business as Kevion approached where Thierry and I were sitting.

"This team captain looking ass nigga," Thierry chuckled. "It's just training camp, relax."

"It's only *just* to you cause you play too damn much," Kevion countered. "Cross out here fighting for his life and you talking about *just* training camp."

Thierry scoffed. "He's been hooping his ass off. You know there ain't shit to worry about. Come on," he ribbed, sitting up. "I know Coach been in your ear. Dream team back together, or…?"

Instead of answering, Kevion just gave him a look, which… *hmmm.*

Kinda felt like an answer.

Kev was a pretty straight shooter, and if he knew something like that was the opposite of true, he would – tactfully -- correct it.

Instead… he was straight-faced now.

Unnaturally so.

Yeah.

There had definitely been talks.

"Cross – Sierra and Janiyah are fucking *pressed* about getting you over for dinner. Janiyah says she needs you for a Tiktok?"

I frowned, shaking my head. "Hell no – she has more followers than me, and them damn teenagers are mean as fuck."

"Tell her yourself – Sierra is getting takeout from Honeybee…"

Still, I shook my head. "Tempting offer, but I think I'm gonna hit the recovery room, then head home. Today took it out of me. Tell them tomorrow though – they have my word."

Kev shrugged. "Okay, but when they start throwing the subliminal shade online about you being ghost, don't say I didn't warn you."

"He can't say *shit*, cause he knows he's been a recluse," Thierry chimed in, earning a side-eye.

Although… he wasn't wrong.

My Summer in the Heights hadn't been *only* about getting out of the spotlight – I *had* withdrawn from my friends in the industry as well. I could admit now that the shit had been hurtful – borderline traumatic if I was keeping it completely transparent. Being so far removed from the team, and team-adjacent friends, have given me space to pretend it wasn't really happening.

Not that it worked that well, but still.

It had been a decent enough exercise in solitude, and what my life might look like if I never got to rejoin the team. I'd even purchased the building, trying to get a foot into a different source of income just in cause I didn't get anymore professional basketball checks, so my savings wouldn't be affected.

Well... *too* affected.

The building needed remodeling, and probably better "maintenance" than Arthur was providing, but he'd come with the building and I didn't have the heart to replace him.

Not that my loyalty got me any damn respect.

"Not too much of a recluse – what's up with shorty you brought to the mixer?" Kev asked, and a grin bloomed on my face before I could school my expression.

"Yeah, you *should* be cheesing, she was bad as fuck – where you find her?" Thierry questioned. "Better yet – are you finished with her?"

"Nigga, don't even play with me like that," I told him, the smile dropping from my face... and he picked that shit right up.

"Ohhhh, she means something to him – you see how serious he got?! Look at his face!" Thierry cackled. "Aye, you got her vetted, right? Or she already got her hands in your pockets?"

Kev scoffed. "You know damn well Cole wouldn't be going for that – as many headlines as she's saved *your* ass from."

Thierry tossed his arms up. "Hey, I *welcome* the villain edit, it don't mean a thing to me." He shifted to toss a smirk in my direction. "I keep trying to tell you – just let them paint you as a bully – keeps people from messing with you."

"In both directions," Kev added on. "Don't get boxed out of endorsements getting influenced by this nigga."

"Me?!" Thierry feigned confusion. "If anything, *Cross* is the bad influence – sleeping with trainers, punching coaches..."

"Wow, not you making it sound like it's a habit?" I

spoke up, laughing. "It was a one-time lapse in judgement."

Thierry sucked his teeth. "You hit *one* time?"

"Fine – seven or eight," I admitted. "But *still* a lapse in judgement. I'm a changed man."

"Not *too* changed, I hope," Kev said. "We need *Crossover Calvin* back in the damn paint. *Bad.*"

I chuckled. "Yeah… I saw the film from those last games of the season."

"Whoa – no shit talking until you've racked up some stats," Thierry said, and I chuckled.

"Fair enough."

We shot the shit a bit longer before peeling off to the showers, and then on to the recovery room for me. Ice baths were never fun, but they made it where you'd actually be able to move the next day, which was good enough for me.

It wasn't until I was heading to my car, leaving the practice facilities, that I was able to check my phone. I had more notifications than I cared more, mostly from social media, which was getting closer by the day to annoying me so bad I just took it all off my phone.

I checked in with my mom, who'd made a habit of sending me a prayer via text every day – not anything she copied from the internet either, *her* words, *her* desires for me, *her* encouragement. I wouldn't front… it actually did a lot for me.

If nobody else was in my corner, her, and my sister?

Always holding it down.

And then there was Amelia.

"Please tell me you made a million goals today. --Li-Li."

That was the text I had from her, immediately brining

a grin to my face once I was settled in the car. It was from nearly an hour ago, so she was probably home and settled as well by now.

"Goals? Please be serious." was all I texted back, knowing I was going to call as soon as I got to my place in Blackwood.

Except, she beat me to it.

"You're focused on the wrong thing, Cross," she said. "Goals, homeruns, whatever – I need some good news."

"What's going on?" I asked, frowning not just at her words, but... *hm*. Something in her voice.

"It has just been... a day. We had an app outage during a walk through with Rori Martin for the integration."

"I thought you were supposed to do stuff like that in a... test environment?" I offered, recalling a conversation we'd had.

"Thank you for the confirmation that you actually listen when I talk," Amelia said. "But, we *were* using a test environment for that... while the live site went down. I was *mortified*. And panicking, because every second we're down, we're losing money, and customer trust, and just *ugh*."

"So it's still down right now?"

"No – Rori helped us figure it out. She's still a developer you know, and she had a major outage issue happen with her app before, so she was able to kind of... calm me down I guess. But those hours while it wasn't working... talk about crying, screaming, throwing up."

"Ah man – I'm glad it's fixed, but that's fucked up. What was the issue – or is that too technical?"

"Above my pay grade," she answered. "I'm just glad they fixed it – and now I have to figure out how to make it right with the customers who were affected by the outage."

"Make it right how?"

"I don't know," she whined. "Discounts, bonuses, groveling apology email? I don't know," she repeated. "This sucks ass. Anyway—you never answered me earlier. How many homeruns today."

"Baskets," I corrected. "And... enough to be pretty sure I'll be in the starting lineup."

"Awww, congratulations! How do you feel?"

"Exhausted. They ran our asses in the ground today – I had to do the damn ice bath."

"Oh nooo," she groaned. "And here I am calling to complain like you don't have your own stuff."

"What? Don't even play with me like that," I chuckled. "Your shit is way worse – and even if it wasn't, it doesn't erase that your day sucked. And you can say that."

"My day fucking *sucked*," she immediately shot back, laughing, even as her voice cracked.

The day's workout was nothing compared to how tight *that* made my chest feel.

"Amelia..."

"Do *not* make me cry again," she fussed, clearing her throat. "I *just* shook the headache off. I'm fine."

"I *know* you don't I believe that."

"Well, I need to believe it, so..."

The wobble in her voice was the only reason I didn't push it.

I let her change the subject.

Let her end the call.

While I was in the parking lot of our building.

I waffled a bit over how she would take me popping

up on her like this – I'd definitely let her believe I was referring to my place in Blackwood when I told her I parked. It could be read as deception, which wouldn't mix well with the hesitance she'd already been feeling about... everything.

I turned the car back on, ready to take my ass back where I was supposed to be.

Then I thought about her voice cracking.

Don't make me cry again.

Damn crybaby.

I shook my head, and turned the car back off.

Went to her door.

And the look on her face when she opened it – her swollen, glossy eyes, the way she flung herself into my arms...

Yeah.

Definitely the right decision.

20 /
amelia

I WASN'T LETTING anything get me down today.

I decided it as soon as I opened my eyes – I was just going to roll with whatever little thing might go wrong.

Starting with the cold water in the faucet not turning on.

Like, that side literally would not give me any water, which baffled even the quick internet search I did, thinking it might be a simple fix.

Fine.

Brushing my teeth in hot water was a departure from my norm, but my teeth were still clean after, so no big deal.

The water refusing to get hot for my shower though… *that* was a pain.

But not the end of the world.

Mystery stain on the jeans I'd planned to put on – no biggie.

Snagging a hole in my favorite sweater with my fingernail, *and ripping the nail too deep into my goddamn nail bed with it…*

I had to sit down for a second after that, to collect myself.

But... a bandaid from the first aid kit in the bathroom, and a quick search for a skilled seamstress on Proxy made everything a little brighter.

I was ready to head to Urban Grind and start my day.

"Good morning Mama," I greeted as I breezed up to her in the kitchen to kiss her cheek... *wait a damn minute.* "Mama?!" I squealed, wrapping arms around her to squeeze. "What are you doing here?!"

"Did you forget about my visit?" she questioned, putting down the knife she'd been using to slice cucumbers at my counter.

"So... yes *and* no," I admitted. "Like, I knew, and even told people about it, but it wasn't like... top of mind. Yesterday was a lot," I sighed, referring to the app outage that had felt like the end of the world.

"I know baby," she said, cupping my face in her hands. "So I'm glad I was already coming. I'm going to make you some fresh pickles."

"Ooooh," I mused, glancing around the kitchen at all her supplies – things I'd clearly tuned out breezing to the bathroom earlier. "You lugged all this stuff up here by yourself instead of calling me?" I fussed. "Also... actually... how did you even get this in here without letting me know you'd made it in?"

She smirked, stepping away to peek into the pot boiling on the stove. "A very, *very* handsome young man, with large arms let me in."

"A... *what*? I... *what?"*

Was... this what dying felt like?

This explode-implode-freezing-burning-overwhelming tightness, jelly-legs, staticky sensation.

198

I was transitioning to the other side.

"Don't start stuttering now," Mama laughed, moving back to slicing the mountain of cucumbers on the counter. "He was very well-mannered – can tell his Mama raised him right. Not like that Hunter boy. Saw *him* too."

Oh.

Okay.

This feeling, where it felt like my skin was turning inside out.

This was the end.

"He just froze – didn't say nothing until I spoke to him. He mumbled something and ran off – didn't even hold the door open for me. Can you believe that?!" he fussed.

"He probably just didn't know how to react, Mama – he thought really highly of you," I assured her. "It's just awkward. These are the cucumbers you were supposed to be bringing to him, right?"

She sucked her teeth. "He can have a jar of pickles – that's all the cucumbers he gets out of me," she said. "And to be clear -- that young man coming out your door right when I was about to knock – *that* was awkward," she corrected, bringing a fresh round of heat to my face. "But he recovered well – straight into gentleman mode. Told me he sees where you get your beauty from," she bragged, and I shook my head.

Because, of course he'd charmed my mother.

He was very, very good at saying the all right things – and *doing* all the right things.

Like showing up at my door the night before.

If he'd mentioned it, I would have surely encouraged him to stay in Blackwood, to rest up from his day.

But *man* was I glad he'd just popped up.

The comfort of his arms, the humor of his commentary, and... the distraction of sex were exactly what I'd needed to wake up optimistic this morning.

I just hadn't expected to walk into... *this*.

"So when were you going to tell me about this young man?" Mama asked. "Was it supposed to be a secret?"

"No," I immediately refuted. "Not... exactly. It's just not like... official yet?"

"Why not? Something wrong with him?"

I chuckled. "No, actually. Everything so far is... pretty right. It's just really soon after Hunter, and... I don't know. I don't want to move too fast."

"Very understandable," she nodded. "Sit down – talk to me about it. Or what, you got something else going on?"

"Nothing that can't wait," I answered. "Let me text Shia real quick though, catch her before she leaves to meet me at the coffee house."

I was *supposed* to be having a sit down to work through the customer service logistics for yesterday's outage – my team, however, wanted me to sit it out. They were insistent on just coming back to me with options, instead of me being super involved... while I was super emotional.

They were probably right, honestly.

I just found it incredibly hard to take that step back and let them get at it.

With my mother being here though... I kinda had to.

So... I dropped that text to Shia, knowing she would actually be relieved to get it, and be able to figure things out with the rest of the team without my overly-neurotic input.

"Okay," I said, once I'd put the phone down. "Where do you need me?"

"Wash your hands first," she said. "Then come on and help me cut up these pickles. You talked to the realtor about your other place?"

For a moment, I frowned, not knowing what in the world she was talking about – that *just* how far removed my *dream brownstone* was from my mind.

"It got completely taken off the market, actually," I answered. "A couple days ago. Chase let me know, and there was so much other stuff going on that it barely registered a blip."

"Well, if you were wrapped up with your new boyfriend, that makes sense."

"Mama!" I laughed. "Calvin was gone to training camp already – I was working on a *business deal*!"

"Tell me anything," she shrugged. "Is that what y'all are calling it these days? We used to say *going to see a man about a horse*. You know, since you ri—"

"*I get it*!" I spoke up from the sink, turning to wrinkle my nose at her. "Can you please not?"

"And *why* not?"

"Because I am *not* grown enough to talk sex with my mother?"

"You was grown enough for that big tall man to let me in here before the sun was up good."

I gasped. "Now how could I have helped that?!"

"Choosing a different day then the one your mother was visiting to get your little feminine itches scratched?"

"*Feminine itches*?!" I shrieked, laughing. "I know what you mean, but that sounds like something else entirely was going on, first of all. Second – I didn't know he was coming. He saw how upset I was about the outage, so…"

"He came to give you something else to think about. Like his penis."

"Mama! He came to *comfort* me!"

"With his penis."

"*Mother, pleeeeassse.*"

"Okay, okay," she laughed. "I'm just teasing you – you know that, right?"

I sighed. "Yes, I know."

"Good. I've only had to worry about you once – I know you'll navigate things just fine."

"When did you have to worry about me?" I asked, frowning.

"When you brought Hunter in my house to introduce him," she answered, immediately.

Like… *so* fast.

"I thought you *liked* him, Mama, it's been years!"

She shrugged. "He was your choice, so I went with it. And he was a nice young man – nothing *wrong* with him. Just… not for you."

Yeah.

Definitely not for me.

"This other young man though – Calvin. I like him."

I smiled. "Yeah… I like him too."

Mama stayed all day.

By the time she was climbing back into her rental, I had a pantry full of homemade pickles that would last a month tops once my friends found out I had them. Mama was headed to Sugar Valley for a retreat – her pop-in with me was a pit stop after flying into Blackwood.

I was really, *really* glad she'd come.

But it felt *so,* so quiet after she'd left.

I followed up with Shia and my team, and actually

ended up blending two of the options they offered for making things right with both the customers *and* the contractors that depended on Proxy. I took a jar of pickles up to Hunter's door, and left them there.

Closure, one last peace offering, closing the loop on me telling him my mother was giving him... whatever it was, I wasn't *quite* sure.

But it felt like the thing to do.

And kinda felt like the way to fully close that door.

As if my mother had spoken it up, I also had a message from Chase, about the brownstone.

My deposit had been returned, and he was wondering if I wanted him to start looking for something else.

Which... *did I?*

As much as I'd wanted that – wanted something fresh and new and *mine*... now I wondered if I'd just needed to break up with Hunter the whole time.

My desire for a brownstone had started back when we were together, as if a fresh space that was *ours* would fix the cracks in our relationship.

He'd hated the idea.

So when we *did* breakup, I'd gone after it full throttle.

At this point, with months of time behind me... would I even still be happy with it?

The apartment I was in now – I *loved* it.

I'd decorated, curated the space, and it was all very *me*. It was the perfect size to have all my stuff and it still felt airy, instead of empty. And it wasn't so big that it felt like a major task to keep clean.

It suited me.

And having Calvin next door is a perk, too.

I grinned to myself.

Was it nice having him right next door, but in *his* space instead of mine?

Uh, yeah.

But I wasn't sure how big of a perk it *really* was, when he was about to be gone anyway, flying and practicing and playing and whatever the hell else professional basketball players did.

Life was about to change for him, as he transitioned back to his team.

He didn't seem too worried about it, which made sense – he was getting back to *his* normal.

But it was all going to be new for me.

Sitting outside on my balcony, I pulled my knees up under my chin and hugged them, staring off into the distant city lights.

Even if it was still pretty new, even if we hadn't *really* put a title on it yet, the reality was still what it was.

I was dating a professional athlete.

One who, in a few weeks, would be the source of headlines, his pictures splashed across a million screens. Lots of attention, lots of scrutiny for him.

And also, potentially... *me.*

Rori had already told me what to do about it – tune it out. Of course, her situation was pretty different, with her story having a lot more drama and mess than any nosy gossip bloggers could *ever* find on me. But it was close enough to resonate with me, and I planned to keep the advice close in my mind.

Kae and Claire's advice was to not overthink it.

Could he be a playboy?

Sure.

I'd only known that man a few months, it would be literally insane to launch myself – my *heart* – full throttle.

But I could enjoy it for what it was, *whatever* that was, from moment to moment, and see what it became.

And the thought of it made me smile.

Like… I literally couldn't keep a grin off my face at the thought of him.

Which kinda contradicted the whole *don't go full throttle* thing, but man… whatever.

I liked him.

I wasn't even surprised when my phone rang and it was his name on the screen, like he knew he was on my mind.

I had the answer button swiped before it could ring a second time.

"What you smiling about?" he asked, making me frown and look around, first at *his* balcony, which was empty.

"How did you know I was smiling?"

"Cause I know you saw my name on that phone before you answered. Why wouldn't you be smiling when a real nigga call?"

"Boy," I laughed, shaking my head. "I'm guessing you're out of practice for the day?"

"Mmmhmm," he groaned, his voice sounding low and sexy and comfortable and… muffled. "Already in my bed – in Blackwood, so you can't get to me."

My eyes went wide. "So *I* can't get to *you*?"

"Mmhmm. You got me in trouble."

"You're gonna have to explain that one."

He chuckled. "Man… I was so damn drained in practice this morning after fooling with you all night."

"And that's *my* fault?"

"Exactly."

"I'm hanging up."

"Don't do that," he pleaded. "I'm messing around – I was almost late because of traffic, but they actually took it easy on us today. They're trying to fake us out -- planning on another grind tomorrow before they make cuts."

"Oh. Damn. That's why you stayed in Blackwood tonight?"

"Yeah – between needing to be fully rested and not worrying about the travel time in the morning. *And...* I didn't know if your mother was staying with you or not. You did *not* warn me about that at all."

I dropped my face into my free hand. "Yeah... about that..."

I took a moment describing the situation from my point of view – waking up to find my mother in my apartment, then realizing how she'd gotten in – and then he explained from his.

"I'm very glad I had already handled my business in the bathroom before I left, because I *surely* would've been standing there shitty if I hadn't," Calvin laughed. "I opened the door and she was already just... *right there,* with your face, looking like *who the fuck are you.* She works in the school system, doesn't she?"

I giggled. "Uh... yes, actually. Thirty years, all the way up the chain."

"Yeah, I know that look *real* well," he cackled. "I could hear the key ring shaking, feel the threat of in-school-suspension just looming over me... and then she smiled at me. Said, *you look nice and sturdy. Come get these bags and tell me about yourself, since you seem so acquainted with my daughter.*"

My eyes went wide. "That is *not* how she characterized it to me. She made it seem... I don't know, breezy!"

"For the most part it was – I like your mom. I think she'd get along with mine well. Maybe *too* well."

I smirked. "Oh… so you're planning on me meeting your mother, huh?"

"I said *they* would get along well. I don't know how she'd feel about *you*."

"What!?"

"Chill," he laughed. "You should know by now I'm—"

"*Just fucking around*," I mimicked his voice, as annoyingly as I could. "Cause you're always playing, cause you play too much."

"You know you like that," he teased. "Anyway – yes, I'm planning on you meeting my mother. Been planning that since those margarita pouches in front of the air conditioner."

I smiled. "Seriously?"

"Yeah, seriously," he said. "It's already lined out – booked your travel for the first game and everything."

My eyes went wide. "Wait, what? You want me to come to your game?"

"Why do you sound surprised?"

"I… I don't know. That's just very… official. And I thought we'd agreed that this wasn't really… a thing?"

Calvin sighed. "Be serious, Amelia. It's definitely a thing. Definitely official."

"You *definitely* decided that on your own," I said.

"I did," he agreed. "And what are you going to do about it? Besides *definitely* getting your ass on that plane and *definitely* sitting next to my mama to cheer me on at this game?"

I sat back.

Still smiling.

"Definitely not a thing."
Except... shit.
Maybe it was?

The end.

and now...

If you enjoyed this book, please consider leaving a review at your retailer of choice. It doesn't have to be long - just a line or two about why you enjoyed the book, or even a simple star rating can be very helpful for any author!

My Website: https://beingmrsjones.com
Instagram: @beingmrsjones
TikTok: @beingmrsjones
Facebook: Romance by CCJ
Newsletter: Sign Up

Check out CCJROMANCE.COM for first access to all my new releases, signed paperbacks, merch, and more!

For a full listing of titles by Christina C Jones, visit www. beingmrsjones.com/books

faces and places

Want to read more about some of the reoccurring characters/places mentioned in this book?

Urban Grind - A Crazy Little Thing Called Love
Winnie - Split Decision
Sugar & Spice Magazine - The Trouble With Love
Wax Poetic - The Reinvention of the Rose
Cole & JJ/RSM - Love on the Highlight Reel
Rori & Sierra, Kevion - Free Agent
Chase the Realtor - Reverb
Fresh - Grow Something
Nectar - Hostile Takeover
Pot Liquor - Fall In Love Again

the ccj reader society

EST **ccj** 2013

CCJ ROMANCE SOCIETY

Love, in Warm Hues

Want early access to new releases, special edition paperbacks, audio before everyone else hears it, serials, and whatever else my little brain thinks of?
Join the CCJ Reader Society on Patreon!

about the author

Christina C. Jones is a best-selling romance novelist and digital media creator. A timeless storyteller, she is lauded by readers for her ability to seamlessly weave the complexities of modern life into captivating tales of Black characters in nearly every romance subgenre. In addition to her full-time writing career, she co-founded Girl, Have You Read – a popular digital platform that amplifies Black romance authors and their stories. Christina has a passion for making beautiful things, and be found crafting, cooking, and designing and building a (literal) home with her husband in her spare time.

the backlist is strong

Need help navigating my backlist?

IN (constant)
DEVELOPMENT

AN EVER-GROWING GUIDE
TO THE PLACES AND PEOPLE
LIVING INSIDE CCJ'S HEAD

CURATED WITH LOVE
BY #TEAMCCJ

Get your FREE copy of In Development, your guide to the
CCJ multiverse!